THAT'S WHAT SHE SAID AT THE PICNIC

(On the Corner of Avenue B and 5th Street)

by

R. Michael Koval

RoseDog❖Books

PITTSBURGH, PENNSYLVANIA 15222

ISBN-10: 0-8059-9070-4
ISBN-13: 978-0-8059-9070-6
Library of Congress Control Number: 2005932439

Printed in the United States of America

First Printing

For information or to order additional books, please write:
RoseDog Books
701 Smithfield Street, Third Floor
Pittsburgh, Pennsylvania 15222
U.S.A.
1-800-834-1803

Or visit our website and online catalogue at www.rosedogbookstore.com

CONTENTS

The author with his dad, Andrew, and his younger brother, Teddy.
Picture taken on Easter Sunday, 1950, on the roof of 77 Avenue B.

PROLOGUE

Bobby and Jerry decided to spend their two-week vacation in New Orleans to hear the jazz and meet some Southern girls. They estimated the drive would take five to six days since there was no rush. That meant at least seven days on Bourbon Street. It was June, 1962. And this is what happened.

CHAPTER I
THE ARRIVAL AFTER THE TRIP

While Jerry went to the head, Bobby sat alone at the bar. It gave him a chance to think about the trip, which had ended about two hours ago. From Avenue B and 5th Street, New York City, to Bourbon Street, New Orleans, in three days. Not too bad since it was a leisurely trip with a stopover in the Smokey Mountains and a night in Tennessee visiting Willie, Vera, Danny, and Helen. The Town and Country Motel was the landing spot before cleaning-up and making a run at Bourbon Street.

Vera, Willie's wife, was something else — a real tiger. Only hours after arriving at their home in Memphis, Bobby commented on the strained relationship between Willie and his younger brother, Danny. Vera responded by slapping Bobby, first across the face and then many more shots all over the top and the sides of his head and extended arms, before she was subdued by Willie and Danny. Helen, Danny's wife, attended to Bobby. It was mostly his pride that was hurt. Jerry remained sitting on the couch, laughing through it all. He had warned Bobby to keep his mouth shut. Willie (Jerry's friend) and Danny (Bobby's friend) were close, but there still was an edge to their relationship. Willie was very motivated and pushed to get ahead, finally succeeding as a top salesman in the carpet company he entered as a stock clerk. Danny was not as aggressive as Willie and much more laid back. Even so, they went into business together in a small supermarket venture, which they said was doing well. It was based on this that Bobby commented on the strained relationship being something of the past when Vera exploded. Maybe all was not well, but Bobby was not going to say anything more, ever again.

Thinking about the Memphis incident, Bobby thought about the first time he had seen Vera's temper. It had been eighteen years ago, plus or minus, in the mid-forties, when Vera battled it out, street fight style, on the corner of 6th Street and Avenue B, with one of the Amazons, a

1

teenager named Lulu — and she was that, a "lulu." Bobby was about ten years old at the time.

The Amazons were an amazing and striking group of young girls. There were maybe six of them, all good looking, and each very tall, close to six feet, either way. The Amazons, as they appropriately called themselves, lived in the same vicinity: Houston, 1st, 2nd and 3rd Streets, between Avenues A, B, and C. Gathered together by coincidence and not a special environment (different air, water, food), the girls joined to form the Amazons. They terrorized other girl groups in the neighborhood, as well as many guys.

In one of their nightly prowls, they got into some words with Vera and her gal pals. It was only a matter of time before they locked horns, because Vera and her friends, while not as tall and statuesque as the Amazons, were quite a formidable-looking group and would not take crap from just anyone. Vera was their leader and had to battle with the main Amazon, Lulu, and it was quite a fight. The ring of men, women, girls, and boys grew larger as word spread. Most of the patrons in the Brown Bear left the bar.

Neither girl backed-off; instead, they punched, swung, kicked, pushed, and pulled hair, knocking over garbage cans, banging into cars, and bouncing off the sidewalks and street. Vera landed the final hard shot that hit the Big One square in the stomach. Lulu doubled over and fell to her knees. Vera, to her credit, did not kick or punch the fallen one. Instead, she lifted her arms in victory, and the partisan crowd broke into cheers for our local girl, the winner, the good sport. After a few minutes of cool-down, the two bloodied warriors shook hands and hugged; thus began a respectful relationship.

And, to think a few years later, Vera marries Willie, and a dozen or so years after that, Vera clobbers Bobby.

As she approached, Bobby remembered her as one of the dancers from the stage behind the bar, a nice-looking blond. She sat down, looked, smiled, and asked, "Will you buy me a drink?"

"Only if it's a beer."

"Oh, c'mon, be a sport."

Jerry got back. "Who is the lady?"

"I just finished dancing and want to have some fun."

"What's your name?" asked Jerry.

"Candy Barr."

Now Candy Barr was a famous stripper, but this one was not her.

"Candy Bar, bullshit! You're more like a Tootsie Roll."

She started yelling and cursing. The bartender suggested the boys leave.

The rest of the day was spent barhopping, with the main event an evening in Convention Hall listening to great jazz played by elderly black musicians who probably started it all. It was also enjoyable visiting the The Famous Door. The musicians mingled with the customers between gigs. The boys had a chance to talk to them about the playing they heard at Nick's in the Village, Central Plaza on 2nd Avenue and 6th Street, Basin Street East on Broadway, and Eddie Condon's place in Midtown — the main jazz joints. Conrad Janus and his trombone were a fixture at the Plaza nearly every Friday and Saturday nights.

Jerry drove his car back to the motel. It was about eleven P.M. when they ordered hamburgers at the restaurant. They reminisced about the trip, the stopover in Memphis being the highlight, if you could call it that. They were glad to arrive safely and were happy with what they saw and heard on their first trip to Bourbon Street. They couldn't wait until it resumed tomorrow. They wondered how the vacation would turn out. Were they in for a surprise.

CHAPTER II
THE MEETING

After a late breakfast at the motel restaurant and a few hours at the pool, the guys went back to "The Street." First they went to Pete Fountain's and listened to the clarinet maestro play his rendition of "When It's Sleepy Time Down South," "Ol' Man River," "Tin Roof Blues," "Stranger on a Shore," and many others. They passed by Al Hirt's on the corner, which was closed for two weeks because he was on tour. They stayed for a couple hours at the Famous Door listening to jazz, jazz, and more jazz, from Dixieland to Chicago to New Orleans. Then Bobby and Jerry decided it was time for girls, girls, and more girls.

Walking down Bourbon, the first strip bar they came upon was Club Paree. The bar area was no different than the joint visited yesterday: A bar with a stage behind it and a pole which the girls wrapped themselves around while dressed only in bikini-style bras and panties. But this place had added features. A dance floor was surrounded by maybe nine booths and a place for an audience of a dozen people, where apparently you could sit and watch the dancing for free. Two rows of six chairs faced the bar and stage area. The boys didn't pay much attention to this section because it was too far away from the bar, the drinks, and even further away from the stage and the dancing girls.

Bobby and Jerry drank beer and watched as girl after girl performed for fifteen to twenty minutes. After dancing, the girls patrolled the bar and audience for companionship in an effort to hustle drinks. These drinks brought an added income to the house, which probably more than paid for the dancing girl's employment. The girls came by, and after being politely told no, they grimaced and smirked, but they did go away.

One girl in particular caught Bobby's eye. She was about 5' 4", well shaped with brown hair in a short bob, which nicely framed her round, attractive face. Her slow dancing manner and casual gaze into the

4

crowd seemed lackadaisical, as if this was a routine that was, well, too much of a routine. Her wandering gaze finally found Bobby's attentive stare, and he was locked into it for what seemed to be many seconds more than her usual gaze time before gliding off into space.

"She really looked at you," Jerry commented.

"Yeah, I can't wait until she makes her rounds," replied Bobby.

Finally, she arrived. "Hello, my name is Norma."

Bobby was shocked. She stood in front of them and extended her hand for a shake, very business-like. He had thought she would bounce across the room and jump into his lap.

"I'm Bobby, and he's Jerry."

"Hello, Jerry and Bobby."

"Sit down and let Bobby buy you a drink," Jerry said with a mischievous smile, "and ask for a mixed drink."

"Why not champagne?" she asked.

At this point Bobby had to speak up. "No way. It's beer or nothing."

Then he thought of the Tootsie Roll incident yesterday and didn't want to lose this one. "Okay, have champagne if you want," he said dryly.

"That's all right. I'll have a beer," she said as she sat down on the stool previously occupied by Bobby.

The bartender didn't like her order the way he sneered, but he served the beers, hers with a glass.

"How long do you work?" asked Jerry.

"Twelve hour shifts with two hours off. Ten to ten, noon 'til midnight. It depends on who wants to work and when."

Jerry continued talking to Norma while Bobby looked at her up-close, confirming that she was, indeed, very good-looking. With that bob haircut, she looked kind of perky—Debbie Reynolds perky—but Norma's brown eyes belied that image. Most times they looked at you tired, not alert. Sometimes they sparkled but then returned to being dull, for instance, after one of Jerry's jokes had passed. Her smile was not a full-face grin like Bobby's, but instead more of a sly one, like Jerry's. She finally turned to Bobby and asked, "Why so quiet?"

"I'm enjoying the view."

Jerry laughed. "There he goes with his bullshit, boyish charm."

Norma laughed and her eyes twinkled. Bobby was embarrassed because Jerry had nailed him again.

"He's just jealous because I get carded every now and then even though I'm twenty-six."

"You're nearly an old man of thirty!" she said.

"Please, you're hurting me," groaned Jerry with a smile.

"Sorry, Pops," she replied with a bigger smile.

5

"And how old are you?" Bobby asked.

"Twenty."

"Really?"

"No, I'm twenty-one."

"Big deal, one year."

"Every girl worries about one year."

"That's what she said at the picnic."

"What did you say?" asked Norma with a puzzled look.

"That's what she said at the picnic."

"Now what the hell does that mean?"

"It's a response that can be made to any comment."

"Show me."

"Okay. Someone says, 'I love you,' and you respond, 'That's what he said at the picnic.' Then you say, 'I have diarrhea,' and I reply, 'That's what she said at the picnic.' You tell me, 'You're the greatest guy I ever met,' and I say to you, 'That's what she said at the picnic.'"

"Ya'll starting to worry me," Norma said with a wry smile.

"I haven't been certified as nuts. At least not yet."

Norma said nothing. She just shook her head. She then grabbed Bobby's hand and squeezed it.

It was during this conversation that Bobby noticed she spoke with a drawl.

"Are you from New Orleans?"

"No. Natchez, Mississippi."

The bartender came over. "More drinks?"

"Yes," Bobby said, "and give the girl a drink of her choice."

"Thanks, I really don't like beer. Ed, let me have the Special, thank you."

The Special? What the hell could that be, thought Bobby.

Jerry asked up-front. "What is a Special?"

Norma replied, "It's a small bottle of champagne. Mountain wants us to push it, and it makes Ed happy because he gets bigger tips as the guys get drunker."

"That'll be six bucks," Ed the bartender said, solving the next question of how much it cost. Five dollars for the Special.

Norma looked at Bobby. "Now Ed will get off my back."

"What do you mean?"

"He was giving me dirty looks from the time I ordered a beer."

"Why did you?"

"I didn't want to sting you right away. Ed, I didn't care."

"Afraid that would scare me off?"

"Yeah," she smiled.

"Who is Mountain?" Bobby asked.

"He's the boss."

"Why is he called Mountain?"

"Because he's a big, fat slob. A real mean..." she didn't finish, but she didn't have to. The look she gave told it all. Mountain was a bastard.

The dancing girl behind the bar rang a cowbell and all the off-duty dancing girls and some patrons started laughing. Even Ed finally smiled.

"What's this about?" asked Jerry.

"It's an inside joke, right?" Bobby commented.

"Yes," said Norma. "See Darlene leading that old man though the door?" There was a doorway in a corner of the dance floor. "She's taking him to one of the backrooms."

"If it's like the backroom of the Lamplighters Club, then we know what's going on," said Jerry of our former neighborhood social club.

"How much is it going to cost him?" asked Bobby.

"Darlene likes to impress Mountain. She maybe already made twenty bucks on Specials since she doesn't finish drinking them. Now she is going for the act. Another fifty to one hundred dollars, depending on what he wants," Norma said with disdain.

One of the girls walked up to Norma and said, "Do you think she'll use one or two Specials now?" they laughed.

"What does that mean?" Jerry asked.

"You really don't want to know," Norma replied.

"Yes, we do," chimed in Bobby.

"It's a woman thing," said Norma's friend.

"What isn't?" Jerry replied with a smile.

"Okay," said Norma, "since you asked. Darlene likes to douche herself with champagne." Everybody laughed. Norma introduced her friend and she started a conversation with Jerry.

They ordered another round of beers, Norma's friend included. Norma was still working on her Special.

Bobby asked, "Do all the girls have to do the back room scene?"

Norma looked hard at Bobby. "Only if they want to work here."

The conversation after that was strained, mostly about the weather (summer, hot and humid; winter, mild with lots of rain), the behavior of the tourists (young guys and gals, crazy; older couples, subdued), Mardi Gras (everyone wild), where the boys were from (New York City), and the mixed drinks they liked (scotch and water).

Jerry finally sounded the bell. "Time to go; I'm burping beer."

"Yes, it's been a long day. What's your starting time tomorrow?" Bobby asked.

"Tomorrow is today. It's one A.M., and I'll be here at noon."

"Until midnight?"

"Yes."

"Okay, I'll be back this afternoon," Bobby smiled.

"That'll be nice. Goodnight." She smiled, slid off the barstool, and walked to the door marked Private, next to the bar. She stopped at the doorway, looked back and mouthed the words, "Thank you," nodded, and then went into the dancers' dressing room.

The boys went back in a taxi to the motel. They stopped at the restaurant for a sandwich, a slice of apple pie, and coffee. It was their first food since the big breakfast. They discussed the scene at the Paree; the girls—especially Norma—and the action going on. New Orleans appeared to be living up to its reputation as a fun-loving town. Then, they retired for the night.

CHAPTER III
THE FIRST DATE

The next day was nearly a repeat of the day before; up late, breakfast, and then lounging at the pool. Today the pool time was only about an hour because Bobby was anxious to get back to the Club. Jerry sensed that.

"Why don't you go to the bar? I'll join you at six P.M. and then we'll go to Antoine's for dinner?"

"Okay, Antoine's sounds great." It was time they had a solid meal. Why not try the tasty French Creole cuisine for which this town was famous?

Bobby got dressed—today a lot nicer: an ironed sport shirt, not a T-shirt, slacks not dungarees, and loafers not sneakers. He called for a cab and waved good-bye to Jerry, who was talking to two girls, recent arrivals, at the pool. Bobby did not stop to introduce himself. Let Jerry tell them who he was and who he was rushing off to see—his Natchez Dancing Wonder. Wow!

Bobby walked into the Paree. It was four P.M., a little later than he had wanted. Since it was afternoon, the place was not as crowded as the night before, but there were a few at the bar, a couple in the audience, and a booth or two occupied. Bobby sat down. The bartender, not Ed, said hello, smiled, and got him a beer.

Someone walked over. It was not Norma.

"How are you?" she asked.

"Okay. Just getting started," replied Bobby as he lifted up his beer. "Want one?"

"No, thanks."

"How about the Special?"

She looked at him and smiled. "You've been here before."

9

"Last night."

"Good, then I should order a Special since you know the score, but I'll be nice. Charlie, a gin and tonic, please." He smiled back.

"Charlie is not Ed." Bobby said.

"What do you mean?"

"Ed never said hello and rarely smiled."

"They're brothers-in-law. Married the boss's two younger daughters, and they don't like each other. Charlie doesn't like his boss much either."

"So they married Mountain's girls?"

"You know a lot about this place. Who did you meet?"

The question startled Bobby. "What do you mean?"

"Anyone who comes back to this place has to have a reason, and that has to be a female one."

"I did meet someone." But Bobby did not want to mention her name, not now anyway, not to someone he didn't know.

"My name is Bobby, and I'm here with my friend, Jerry, for a week of jazz and female companionship."

"You came to the right town. Where are you from?"

"New York, Lower Manhattan. Avenue B and 5th Street. You?"

"We were neighbors across the river. Astoria, Queens. My name is Josephine. Nice to meet you."

Bobby wondered about her. She dressed very nicely. She was definitely not a dancer—not because she did not have good features and a decent body, but she was a little too old, in her late thirties or early forties, with a tired, beat-up look. Unless she was wealthy and enjoying a day at a bar, there was only one occupation she could easily fit, this time, this place.

"You still thinking about who I'm seeing?" Bobby asked.

"Yes."

"Darlene."

"No. No way."

"Why not?"

"You're not her type."

"Why not?"

"When I first came over, her type would have grabbed my ass."

"Is she that aggressive?" said Bobby with a chuckle.

"She is more than that. A tramp. She does tricks that even make me blush," Josephine smiled and winked at Bobby.

"You're okay, Josephine."

"So, who is it?"

"I'm afraid to say."

"I don't blame you. Mountain does not like some of his girls dating patrons."

"Why? They're just employees."

"No, it's more than that. He likes to believe they're his property, also." Josephine had a disgusted look on her face.

"Well, because of what you just said and since we were once neighbors, I think I can trust you. It's Norma."

At that, Josephine smiled. "She's a sweetheart. Real nice, and she doesn't take Mountain's shit. She fights back. Sometimes too much."

As if on cue, who walks over but the Natchez Flame.

She nodded. "I see you've met."

"Yes, we were just discussing the highlights of the Club." Josephine said with a smirk.

"When do you start dancing?"

"In about an hour."

"Want a drink?"

"Yes, I'll have coffee. Black, no sugar."

"You sure?" Bobby said as he looked in the direction of Charlie.

"It's okay. Charlie's not Ed, and Mountain won't be back until tonight—late, I hope."

"I'll have a coffee, also," Josephine said. "Black, like Norma's."

Bobby placed the order. After some small talk, Josephine left to strike up some business, and they were alone.

"What are you and Jerry planning?"

"Jerry will be here around 6 P.M., and we're going to dinner, then I'll be back."

"Don't come back here. Wait for me outside. When I get off at midnight, I'll turn right and walk along Bourbon. After a block, and if I'm still alone, catch up to me, okay?" All she said seemed so sinister and alarming.

"Whatever you say. See you later."

Bobby was afraid to smile, fearing that if he did, Mountain would somehow drop down on him from the ceiling.

Norma got up, smiled, nodded, and walked away.

Bobby ordered another beer. When he paid, he left Charlie a five dollar tip, meant to say, "This is a bribe." Charlie was very appreciative, and he smiled and nodded in a way that Bobby knew he would keep quiet. Charlie obviously liked Norma and Josephine as much as he disliked Ed and Mountain. Enough said.

While waiting for Jerry, Bobby watched the dancers and then had another chance to talk to Josephine, who returned after a tour of the bar.

"Is there anything special that I could buy for Norma?"

"How about a drink?"

"Be serious."

"Okay, what for?"

"In about five days, or maybe sooner depending on the money flow, we'll be leaving for home. I would like to get Norma something to remember me. Something, you know, she would appreciate."

"One second you're telling me that money flow may cut your vacation time, and now you want to spend it on a gift?"

"Hey, I'm not talking about buying her a car or diamond necklace. How about clothes?"

"How romantic," said Josephine as she rolled her eyes.

"C'mon, think of something."

"I don't know, now but I'll ask her, in a round-about-way, don't worry, and I will tell you what I find out."

"Good. If I don't see you, please call me at the Town and Country and leave a message, okay?"

"Fine. By the way, how did you pick the Town and Country?"

Bobby didn't want to admit it was dumb luck, a chance pick. He wanted to appear the trip was planned. Why? Ego.

"A very good friend recommended it."

"He is, indeed, a very, very good friend."

"And, what is that suppose to mean?"

"He was right, it's a very nice motel." She smiled and nodded.

"Yes, and it's well managed, clean, and friendly. It's large enough to have switchboard operators. The restaurant is also open twenty-four hours, and the price is right!"

"How much?"

"Fifteen dollars a person, twenty-five dollars a room with two."

"That is good considering this is the summer season."

"What does the Hilton charge?"

"Starts at twenty-five dollars."

"If it works out and we're still in town, plan on coming over this weekend and enjoy the pool."

"I'll see. Thanks."

"And thank you for helping with Norma's gift. Remember, something special."

"Yes, a blouse," chuckled Josephine.

"Stop busting my chops. I want her to have nice memories of our paths crossing, our meeting."

"So, you don't see a long term relationship?"

"Should I?"

"Absolutely not!"

"Why?"

"Because she's a country girl. Much wiser than she was two years ago, but still...."

"So, you're going to protect the country bumpkin from the city slicker?"

"No. You're both nice people. Don't confuse this. Listen, I've been here nearly ten years and I can see the difference. Don't try to mix the cultures, understand?"

At this time, Jerry arrived. "I'm going to have a beer. How about you and your lady friend?"

"Jerry, meet Josephine, the Astoria Flash."

"Bobby's the guy who loves nicknames. Hello, Flash."

"Nice meeting you, City Slicker. How are you doing?"

"Enjoying the music and the booze. Met a girl at the motel today and we'll be spending time together tomorrow. Sandy has a girlfriend who would like to meet Bobby, but he is already spoken for."

"Yeah," said Josephine, "really spoken for in so many ways." She smiled at Bobby.

Please, Bobby thought, *please don't say anything to Jerry about me buying Norma a gift. Not at this time, please.*

"Norma feels good about seeing Bobby—at least that what she tells me."

Whew! That was close. Thanks, Josephine.

Norma started dancing about the time they were leaving. Bobby looked at her, and she was in her trance-like state, just going through the motions.

"Good night, Josephine. Hope to see you again." Jerry nodded.

"Sounds good to me. Have a fun night."

The meal at Antoine's was great, definitely worth it. Good to get off the scrambled eggs, meatloaf sandwiches, and hamburger and cheese menu.

They went back to Bourbon Street and to the Convention Hall. In one area of the building, the ground floor, they had a play going on. It was about the old South, the Civil War, and pro-slavery. Too much for the Northern-raised boys, so they returned upstairs to the jazz band for a couple hours of joy. They ended up at the Famous Door, where Bobby left Jerry.

At about ten to midnight, Bobby waited across the street for Norma to leave the Paree. Fifteen minutes later, she exited, turned right, and started walking toward the Famous Door on the corner. She crossed the street, and Bobby followed her for about another block. He checked to see if Norma was alone, then crossed over. He caught up to her and grabbed her by the arm, startling her.

"You scared me." Norma stopped and turned to Bobby.

"Sorry. There was no one following you." Bobby moved with Norma from the sidewalk to a doorway for more privacy.

"Mountain did not come back tonight from wherever he went. If he was back, he probably would have kept me overtime."

"Why?"

"Because he didn't like what he heard about us last night."

"Who complained?"

"Ed, of course, and some of the girls who like to kiss his ass."

13

"About what?"

"Ed complained about the drinks—not enough Specials and you guys drinking only beer. They saw us holding hands and overheard some of our conversation, which Mountain said was too personal."

"So, you're not suppose to get interested in anyone, or is it just cheap me?"

"It's anyone."

"Does he abuse you?"

"No, not physically. He once came close to hitting me, but he didn't. He wanted me to do certain things with him and some of his friends, but he doesn't push it anymore."

"What do you mean, 'doesn't push it anymore'?"

"Forget it, okay? Let's go for a walk. It's a nice night."

"Would you like to stop somewhere to eat or drink?"

"No, thanks. I had enough to eat and too many drinks already. Let's take a walk to the river."

"Neat. I've never seen the Mississippi up close—only drove over it on the long bridge to New Orleans."

"You won't see it tonight either. There's a full moon, but the river will look like black water."

"How far is it?"

"About ten blocks. I never counted."

They started walking, and Bobby grabbed her hand. Norma turned and smiled. The crowd thinned out as they got closer to the river until there was no one else on the street. Across from Norma's favorite dock was a church on top of a hill. The steeple was all lit up and it sort of looked like a lighthouse facing the waterfront. They walked down the wood deck to the end, where there was a little shack, a "bait for sale" place. There was a bench, and Bobby and Norma sat down to rest.

"Do you come here often?"

"I try to make it once a week. It gives me a chance to shake off the Club and think about the things I miss."

"What's that?"

"My momma, my aunt, and my boys." Just as she said "boys," she abruptly turned to Bobby. Her face, lit up by the moonlight, had a pained look. "Please, don't ask me about my boys, not now."

Bobby was stunned. He never expected her to have one child, let alone two.

He stood, clutched Norma's arms, and lifted her up. He wrapped his arms around her. Norma put her head on his chest and started to cry, not heavily, just sobbing.

"Hey, relax. It's not the end of the world."

"I screwed-up so bad. I'm trying to get it together. Sometimes it seems like it's working, and sometimes it seems impossible."

14

"Norma, please stop beating yourself up. Don't think about anything. Just keep hugging me, okay?"

After a while she pulled away. Bobby offered her his hanky. She dabbed her eyes and cheeks.

Norma looked at Bobby with her sad eyes, as sad as he imagined they could be. "Is my mascara running?"

"A little, but you still look beautiful."

She smiled and again put her head on his chest and her arms on his shoulders.

"Do you realize, Norma, we've known each other for nearly two days now, and we haven't even kissed?"

"Is that supposed to be a record for you?"

"As a matter of fact, yes. Usually it's only hours."

"Not for me. Usually it's minutes."

"Tramp."

She laughed and gave Bobby a big hug. Then they looked at each other and finally kissed.

At first it was tender. Then she slowly began to move her mouth. She pressed harder and her lips moved faster. Bobby relaxed just a little, and she reacted with even more force. Her mouth was wide open and her tongue was everywhere. With her passion at full steam, Bobby felt as if she was trying to swallow his head. He dropped his hands from her back down to her ass and lifted her even closer to him. He started to get hard and she felt it. Now her body gyrated into his. Finally, Norma broke the suction. She pressed her face against his chest.

"Wow! That was great. Thank you," sighed Bobby.

"It's been a long time since I've kissed someone I liked."

"How would it be if it was someone you loved?"

"You can't imagine it."

She was right, he couldn't. Not after what he just experienced.

They stayed embraced and the passion remained.

"Since the mood is still here, do you want to go to your apartment?"

"No, my roommate has her boyfriend living with us. It's too crowded."

"Let's go to my motel. If there's a vacancy, we'll take it. If not, there's my room and a twin bed. Jerry is a heavy sleeper, especially when he's tanked. Is that okay with you?"

"Of course, anywhere but here. I don't want splinters in my ass." She smiled and Bobby agreed.

A few blocks later they caught a cab. The motel's NO VACANY sign was posted. They quietly entered the room. Jerry was fast asleep. They undressed and slipped under the covers. The passion was renewed.

15

CHAPTER IV
THE BREAKFAST AND THE LUNCH

Jerry rolled over. Norma's back was to him, but Bobby had a direct look, and he watched. Jerry awoke and sat up. He looked to his left and saw Norma in Bobby's bed. "Oh, shit," he said and fell back.

"Don't worry, Jerry, I won't attack you," teased Norma. Bobby laughed.

Jerry stretched and tried to be cool. "What time you get in?"

"About one-thirty. You were really out."

"What time is it?" asked Norma.

"Eight-thirty."

"When do you have to check in?" asked Bobby.

"Two."

"I'm going to watch some TV before I shower, okay?" said Jerry as he got up and clicked on the TV.

"Sure, Jerry, just don't peek," said Norma as she snuggled into Bobby's arms.

While Jerry showered, Norma got out of bed, put her right forefinger on top of her head and spun around, slowly.

"You are very well proportioned," Bobby said while watching Norma with eyes very wide open.

"Thank you, but you didn't say I was pretty?"

"That's obvious. What's your middle name?" quizzed Bobby.

"Mary, after my mother's sister."

"You sure it isn't Jean?"

"Why?" she frowned.

"Well, you know, Norma Jean Baker Monroe, like in Marilyn?"

"Stop it!"

"Well, you are pretty and well-built."

"But I'm not Marilyn, okay?"

"Don't get pissed at me. I meant it as a compliment."

Norma smiled. "All right." She kissed him on the cheek and pulled him over her.

After Jerry got out of the shower, Norma, wearing Bobby's robe, went into the bathroom. Bobby asked Jerry what he was going to do that day.

"I'm having lunch with Sandy and then, who knows? And you?"

"Well, I'm free for the day since I won't be seeing Norma until two A.M., if that's what she wants."

"Okay, I'll tell Sandy to tell her girlfriend to meet us for lunch."

"I don't know," said Bobby.

"What's the matter? You don't even know her."

"And after I meet her, then what?"

"I'm not asking you to marry her. Just make Sandy happy that her friend has someone to talk to, nothing else."

"Okay, but nothing else."

"Right."

When they arrived at the motel restaurant, Bobby noticed the same large corner table in the back was occupied. No matter what time of day, it always seemed to be in use. *Popular spot for business associates*, Bobby thought.

They ordered, were served, and had polite conversation. Bobby knew Jerry would not mention the blind date, but he still felt guilty. He didn't want to get involved with even talking to another girl. He didn't want to screw with the differing emotions. He wanted to stay on target, and Norma was the one to target on.

Jerry excused himself to use the restroom and Bobby turned to Norma. She had a napkin in front of her face and was picking her nose.

"What the hell are you doing?"

"I tried to blow it out, but it's annoying the shit out of me."

"I have a sinus problem, so I know how you feel, but not in public!"

"I'm sorry," she said after she removed the snot and wiped it in a tissue.

Bobby, exasperated, said, "You know, let's not get too familiar. I don't want us to start farting in front of each other, okay?"

"That won't happen unless you start getting ugly."

Jerry got back. He could sense the tension. "Everything okay?"

"Yeah, let's wrap it up. We're on vacation, but Norma has to work. She's the breadwinner." The boys smiled. Norma didn't.

Bobby drove to her apartment. "This is the first time I've been behind a wheel since we arrived on Tuesday. It's been cabs and more cabs."

Norma was not talking.

17

"What's wrong?" Bobby asked.

"Nothing."

"Yeah, right."

"I'm sorry I upset you," she shook her head.

"Is that what's bothering you?" said Bobby, knowing full well it was. "Forget it, okay, no problem. "

She touched his arm. "Will you come to the Club?"

"I don't think I should show up, do you?" Bobby asked.

"Meet me outside at two, okay? If you want, we can walk to the river."

"Sure, I'd like that."

Norma directed Bobby into a residential neighborhood and had him pull over in front of a private house with a nice lawn.

"My apartment is on the second floor. I share it with my girlfriend, Mary Lou, and her visiting, pain-in-the-ass boyfriend, Billy. Want to come up?"

Bobby knew she was just being polite. "No, I'd better get back. You have to get ready for work."

"See you later."

She looked happy as they kissed.

He watched as she walked away. Her round bottom slowly swayed under her gingham dress. She also had great legs. *What a combination,* he thought.

When Bobby returned to the motel, he passed by the restaurant and realized it was nearly time for lunch. How was he going to eat again so soon after breakfast? Jerry was waiting for him.

"When did you say you were meeting Sandy?"

"Noon time."

"That's only a half hour from now."

"So what?"

"And how am I supposed to eat again? I should have thought about that before I ordered that big breakfast earlier."

"You don't have to stuff yourself. Say you have an upset stomach and order a poached egg and toast. You can handle that, right?"

"You?"

"I'll order two scrambled eggs."

"Okay, let me wash up and we'll go."

When they reached the pool area, the girls were sitting at a table, under an umbrella, sipping what looked like ice tea.

"Hello," said Jerry. "Bobby, meet Sandy and Mary Jane."

"Hi. Is that ice tea or bourbon you're drinking?"

"Too early for bourbon. Is that what you drink?" asked Sandy. A striking-looking blonde, she was slender, wearing a halter-top and shorts.

"Usually it's beer, but when I go heavy, it's scotch and water."

"What brand?" inquired Mary Jane, a pretty brunette. She was shorter than Sandy and a little chubby, also wearing a halter-top but with slacks. Jerry selected well.

"What are you doing, a survey?" Bobby shot back with a smile.

"No," she laughed, "but they say you can tell a lot about someone by what they drink."

"Does J and B rate high?"

"That's good, I'm sure."

"Actually, after a few I can drink the house rot-gut and not know the difference."

They talked for a while, which Jerry and Bobby appreciated since it was more time from breakfast.

The waitress looked quizzically at the boys; she had served them at breakfast just a couple of hours ago. Bobby looked at her, rolled his eyes, and smiled. She smiled back, shook her head, and took the order.

"What would you girls like to do today?" asked Jerry.

Wait a minute, thought Bobby. *What's this "we" crap, Kimosabe?*

Before the girls could reply, Bobby said, "I'm pretty much hung-over and would appreciate just laying by the pool." He smiled at the girls and glared at Jerry.

Sandy agreed, "We were out late as well and would like to rest up for tonight."

Tonight? thought Bobby. He felt a headache coming on, and he would pull that one later in the day.

Most of the conversation centered on the girls, where they lived (Chicago), what they did (worked together at the phone company as secretaries), and what they liked (movies and summer trips to various fun places). Sandy was nice to talk to. She listened and spoke accordingly. Mary Jane was all over the place. She talked as if she were vaccinated with a phonograph needle. The only thing that made listening to her acceptable, and not life threatening, was that she had a very comforting voice. She said she could sing, and that was believable.

After nearly two hours, they left the restaurant, went to their respective rooms, changed into swim gear, and returned to the pool, which was pretty crowded considering it was a Friday afternoon. Jerry and Bobby got some lounge chairs and they grouped together.

"Would you like suntan lotion on your back, Bobby?"

"Yes, thanks, Mary Jane."

Everyone got a coating and turned over every fifteen minutes or so, trying to bake evenly in the sun. After an hour Bobby went into the pool to cool off. When he got out, Mary Jane asked, "More lotion?"

"No, thanks. I've had enough. I'm going for some shut-eye. My head is still banging from last night."

"I've got aspirin." Mary Jane offered.

"I took some this morning, thanks anyway. A little rest should do it. See you guys later."

Bobby was about to shower when the phone rang.

"Hello."

"Bobby?"

"If I'm starting to sound like Jerry, I'm in trouble, Norma. Are you okay? Anything wrong?"

"No, no, honey. I'm fine. I'm calling because I've got good news—I got the day off."

"How did that happen?"

"Mountain is not here, and I told Ed I was having women problems, you know, and he said I should take the day off."

"Did he believe that?"

"He does because a couple months ago I had a really bad case. I was in agony and everybody knew it. He was happy to see me leave."

"Good acting. Did you have to hold your stomach and groan?"

"No, silly. I just looked like I look at least once a month."

"Enough said. Hey, we can go to dinner at Pete Fountains if you'd like?"

"That sounds good. I've never been there."

"Where are you now?"

"I'm calling from a gas station. I'm nearly home."

"It's 3:30 now. I'll pick you up at 5:30 in front of your house. Do you want me to call you first?"

"I don't have a phone. That's enough time. See you soon, honey."

"Sure enough, bye."

Bobby was energized. Time to pull out the suit, the white shirt, tie, and dress shoes. *Oh, shit*, he thought. He had forgotten to tell her to dress up for tonight. Not a gingham dress, but evening attire. *I wonder if she owns anything like that?* he thought. Then he realized what he was thinking. He remembered what Josephine warned him about, the different cultures. Now he was measuring her by his standards of what dressing-up meant. Comparing clothes. He was ashamed. Whatever she wore would be fine. She always looked good in whatever she wore, and he would not comment on it.

Jerry walked in while Bobby was getting dressed. It was nearly five P.M.

"Where are you going?"

"Norma called. She got the day off," no explanation why, "and we're going to dinner at Fountains."

"You got over that headache fast."

"Of course. What are your plans?"

"Sandy and I are going out. Probably eat at Antoines, and then just run around. Mary Jane was hoping you'd get over your headache and take her out with us."

"I was afraid of that. Listen, I don't want to hurt her feelings. Tell her I'm not feeling well and went to sleep."

"That's okay, as long as she doesn't insist on seeing you—you know, wanting to play Florence Nightingale."

"Well, keep her out. Tell her I may be coming down with the flu."

"Yeah, and then Sandy will be afraid to go out with me."

"Okay, okay. Tell them I got a call from a friend and we went to dinner. After all, that's the truth."

"Should I mention, if asked, that the friend is female?"

"Say I just mentioned a friend and did not say who. It's only a little white lie. Isn't that what she said at the picnic?"

"Let's hope we don't run into each other on Bourbon Street."

"I wouldn't worry about that. Norma's had her fill of seeing Bourbon. After Fountain's, we'll go somewhere else."

A little after 5 P.M. Bobby left the room after calling a cab. He checked in the direction of the girls' room, which was about a dozen doors down. No action, and they weren't in the pool area. He walked away without looking back.

CHAPTER V
THE DINNER

The cab pulled up, and Norma was waiting on the sidewalk. Bobby was very surprised. God, did she look good. She had on a black dress with a nice scoop neckline, snug fitting but not tight, knee length. Norma accented her outfit with a pearl necklace and earrings, a small black clutch bag, and black dress shoes with a medium heel. Bobby got out and kissed her on the cheek. Norma wanted it on the lips.

"No, don't mess your make-up, we'll do that later. You look great, kiddo."

"Thank you, Bobby."

He couldn't take his eyes off her during the trip to Fountain's. He couldn't get over how beautiful she looked. She had on the right amount of make-up: hardly any.

"You surprised?"

"Yes, to be honest. I knew you would dress up," he lied, "but you look outstanding. You look like you've just stepped out of *Vogue Magazine*."

She smiled, and Bobby could tell she was proud.

"The pearls are elegant."

"That's because they're real. They were a present from my Aunt Mary. She said I would need them someday in New Orleans. This is the first opportunity I had to wear them, along with my new outfit."

"And it is the right occasion," Bobby noted.

Although they didn't have a reservation, they didn't wait long before they were seated. Norma looked around, fearing that she would know someone and vice-versa. Bobby tried to comfort her by reason: most of the patrons were tourists and the remaining were locals who probably never frequent the Paree. After sweeping the floor for a third time, she finally relaxed. The waiter came over. Norma looked at him, but they didn't know each other.

"Drinks, sir?"

"Yes. Would you like your Special, dear?"

Norma gave him a drop-dead look. "No, I'll have a scotch and water for a change, sweetheart," she said between quenched teeth.

"Make that two J and B's with water, please."

"Thank you. Would you like to order now? I'll give you the Specials."

"There's that word again," Bobby chuckled. He looked and smiled at Norma. She just glared back.

"What word, sir?" asked the waiter.

"It's nothing. We have time before we order, thank you."

"I'll be right back with your drinks."

"You say Special one more time and I swear I'll hit you. I don't want to be reminded of that place, okay?" she hissed.

"All right, I just thought I'd make you feel at home—don't you dare!"

Norma had picked up her purse and made a throwing motion toward Bobby. She didn't mean it, but she had a sneer on her face and Bobby knew he had better knock off anymore references to her job.

"Sorry. No more shop-talk, okay? And what's this with the scotch and water? I thought you liked bourbon?"

"I do, but you mentioned last night that you liked scotch and water, so I thought I'd go along with you."

"That's a nice gesture, thank you."

The house photographer stopped by. "Hello, my name is John. Would you like a picture to remember the evening? It's only five dollars for one, and three dollars for additional prints."

Bobby looked at Norma. "What'da you say, tootsie?"

"Whatever you decide, sweetie."

"Make it two, okay, John?"

"Yes, sir."

They posed, Bobby putting his left arm around Norma, and they smiled.

The drinks arrived, and they ordered dinner. Then they made their first toast.

"To a happy life."

"Yes," she simply replied, and her eyes were shining.

Their glasses clinked and they both leaned toward each other, with Bobby getting up slightly, and they kissed. They drank slowly, eyes locked.

They both ordered filet mignon with a baked potato and a salad. Bobby was trying to think of what to say. He didn't want to upset Norma. She was in a good mood.

"Hey," she said unexpectedly with a big smile, "I've got good news, again."

"What's that?"

"Tomorrow is my day off. Want to go on a picnic?"

"Sure, why not," more an exclamation, not a question.

"I'm going to ask Mary Lou and her boyfriend, Billy, to join us, okay?"

"If you don't mind them, then why should I," again, not a question, but a statement.

"I feel bad because I've been on them about Billy staying as long as he has."

"How long?"

"Well, he came here two months ago just for a visit, then he decided to stay and find a job. He's supposed to move when he finds one."

Bobby interrupted. "And he hasn't found one because he hasn't really been looking, right?"

"How did you know?" she asked with a shit eating grin.

"Because you wouldn't be upset with him if he had been looking."

"Yes, and I feel sorry for Mary Lou. He's living off her, does nothing to help and is a pain. In fact, I disconnected the phone because he was using it so much."

"How do you get urgent messages?"

"I gave my neighbor's number to my mama, Josephine, and Mountain. They're the only ones that would need me. When Billy leaves, I'll probably get a phone, but it's been so nice not getting calls at all hours from people you don't know."

"Hey, why not find him a job at Parees? He can be Mountain's clean-up guy, the go-for-the-Special man."

Norma just looked at Bobby and shook her head in disgust.

"Oops, sorry. Tried a little black humor there and it failed."

"Bobby, you can be so sweet, but sometimes you say things to be funny, and they hurt. You just don't realize how mean you can sound."

Bobby was stunned. Now who's the country bumpkin, he thought.

The waiter came over, just in time for a cool-off period. "Another round? Mr. Fountain is getting ready for the next session and we're not permitted to serve during the playing."

"Of course, bring two each please."

"Yes, sir."

Bobby looked at Norma with woeful eyes. "I'm really sorry, Norma. You're right. I can be really nice, I know, but then I forget feelings and step out too far. I know that, too. I promise to be more careful, okay? Please forgive me for being so inconsiderate."

Norma looked at Bobby and realized he was sincere. His eyes were shining. She smiled, got up, and walked over to give him a kiss on the cheek. He was shocked and pleased. He was also happy to see she was relaxed and not worrying about who would know her.

"If you behave, I'll give you one on the lips later," she threatened, and he loved it. He squeezed her hand. He had to change the subject. He was getting hard.

"By the way, do you get off every Saturday?"

"No. Days off depend on how many girls are available for all the shifts. Summer is good because it's tourists' time and everyone wants to work as much as possible. I asked for Saturday off last Monday, and Mountain said it was okay since that's a weekend and even more tourists, so everyone was available."

"And of course, you had a feeling I was coming."

"No, I just wanted a day to goof off, and I can still do it with you."

"Don't you dare say it."

"What?"

"Goof off with a goof off."

"Honey, I could never be as mean as you used to be," she said emphatically.

"Yes, those bad old days. I won't remember them well," he smiled.

She nodded back. "Well said."

The waiter arrived with the drinks just before Mr. Fountain came on stage, thanked everyone for coming, made a few jokes and then started playing.

They listened quietly, not saying a word, just exchanging glances. When he finished a number, they clapped and she would ask, "What's the name of that one?" Most times Bobby would know, but some tunes he couldn't remember, so he just shrugged.

Nearly an hour later the session ended, and the waiter came over.

Bobby asked, "Another round?"

Norma nodded yes.

"Another round, please, and bring the check."

"Yes, sir. Thank you."

"It's our anniversary."

"Congratulations." He left.

"What anniversary?"

"Our second night together. Forget already?"

"I didn't think it would last." They both laughed.

John, the photographer, returned with the pictures. Norma and Bobby looked at them and nodded their approval. Bobby paid John. John put the pictures, with framed enclosures, into an envelope and put it on the table.

"The picture looks nice," she said.

"How about the music, did you enjoy it?"

"It's different than the country style I'm used to, but it's enjoyable. You really like it, don't you?"

"Yes, I love the clarinet. I'm a Benny Goodman fanatic. I tried to master the instrument for nearly four years, until I was twelve. That's when I heard Benny play, 'Hora Staccato,' and I realized I could never play like that, so I quit. Jerry, Willie, John, and Fats used to baby sit for me and my younger brother, Teddy. They were older by at least five years, and I'd play the clarinet for them."

"Now you and Jerry are friends?"

"Of course. We all grew up together and got to know each other. Age didn't matter anymore."

What Bobby didn't tell Norma was that Jerry and his friends used to make Bobby play the clarinet on purpose, sometimes until he cried. Kids can be the worst tormentors. But they did grow-up in the same neighborhood, and well, bygones will be bygones, forgive and forget. Bobby could not tell Norma. Why make Jerry look like a thug? Jerry was his buddy, a Korean War vet.

"You said you're from New York City?"

Bobby nodded yes.

"Why don't you have an accent?"

"My parents came to the City from Pennsylvania during the Depression. I spent nearly all my summers with my Uncle Johnny, Aunt Lottie, and Butchie in Wilkes-Barre, my folk's hometown. So, my accent is part City and part Pennsly-tucky."

"So you got all of your schooling in New York?"

"Yes. Public Schools #71 and #64, Brooklyn Automotive High, and Brooklyn Polytechnic."

"You went to college?"

"Yes."

"Oh, you're a scholar!"

"No, not at all. I learned enough to make a decent living. "

"What do you do?"

"I'm a mechanical engineer, working for a consulting firm."

"Sounds interesting."

"Most times. The best part is seeing your air-conditioning design being built, installed, and tested."

The waiter arrived with the drinks. Bobby signed the charge slip and gave it back to the waiter.

"Thank you, and again, congratulations. Enjoy.".

"Enjoy?" Bobby mimicked. "I think our waiter might be Jewish."

"Why?"

"Usually when you say 'enjoy' only, it's like saying 'Shalom,' a simple word that means a lot."

"Are you Jewish?"

"No, I'm Roman Catholic."

"I shouldn't be talking to you. I'm a Southern Baptist."

"Let's make a truce."

"After last night, why not?"

This time Bobby squeezed Norma's hand, "Okay. Peacetime."

You asked me about schooling. What about you?"

Norma looked away, "I didn't finish high school. I only went one year."

"I'm surprised. You speak very well, have a good sense of humor, quick retorts, and you had no formal education?"

"I may be from Natchez, but they do have libraries there and here, in New Orleans. I read a lot. That's been my 'formal' education. I enjoy reading very much; it takes me away from it all."

"I bet. It's funny, but most people I know buy their books. They only go to the library for research."

"You one of them?"

"Yes."

"I couldn't afford all the books I've read. I also enjoy movies."

"You go often?"

"No, not too much because the movies I like they hardly make any-more. I sometimes see them on television."

"What type of movies?"

"Movies where they talk back to each other. Like, *The Thin Man*, *Adam's Rib*, *His Gal Friday*. The only ones lately are the Rock Hudson and Doris Day films."

"Now I know where you get your sense of humor and how your per-sonality was influenced. Nobody did it better than Powell and Loy, Tracy and Hepburn, Grant and Russell."

"Oh," she squealed. "You like them also!"

"They're some of my favorites."

"No wonder we get along so well," she smiled.

They finished their drinks, walked through the restaurant, with Norma not as nervous as before, and got outside.

"I don't want to walk the street."

"Whatever you say," replied a relieved Bobby.

"Can we go to your place?"

"No. Jerry's going out with this girl, Sandy, and they'll probably be using his bed tonight."

"So what? We won't bother them."

"But Sandy may not be comfortable."

"So what? Give her a towel or a robe. If she's still shy, she can ask us to close our eyes."

"Hey, Norma, not everyone's a sport like you."

"What does that mean? I have no feelings? I don't care? I'm a slob?"

"C'mon. Jerry and I don't mind a third party. Girls are different. So you think like a guy. That doesn't mean you're immodest."

"Bobby, you can really pile it on."

"But it's true."

Norma smirked at him.

"Okay, let's go to your place and see if Mary Lou gets upset."

"Funny, but we do have separate bedrooms. If anyone will get upset, it will be Billy."

"Screw him. You're worried about a free-loader?"

"Okay, I'll be honest. The apartment is clean because that's the one main thing Mary Lou and I agree on; we are clean freaks. Billy is a slob, so we try and control him."

"So, what's the problem?"

"We wash our clothes a lot, so we have clotheslines crossing all over the kitchen and living room. It just looks ugly."

"Do you have clean sheets?"

"Of course. We hang them in the living room where the lines are highest."

"Is your toilet clean?"

"Depends on who uses it. We watch Billy on this one."

"So, why can't I go to your place?"

"I'm being selfish. I just like that motel you're in."

"Okay, maybe tomorrow night. I'll check with Jerry."

They got into a taxi and went to Norma's after she called to tell Mary Lou we were on our way. It was nearly eight P.M., late twilight time, when the cab drove up to the house. The place that Norma called home was the second floor of a private house located about a mile from Bourbon Street. It had a separate entrance, a stairway on the side of the house that ran alongside the driveway that lead to the garage in the back. The house was painted a tan color with dark brown trim and a screened front porch facing a nice grass yard. The place looked well kept.

As they entered the apartment, Bobby thought he was looking out his Lower Eastside bedroom window into the courtyard space between the tenements. The room was crossed with a series of clothes lines, not very long, that strung from different door jams to window frames, upon which hung sheets, pillow cases, towels, and such. They maneuvered through the living room into the kitchen, which had only two clotheslines that took care of the smaller gear—all types of underwear, socks and stockings.

Norma noticed Bobby looking at the maze and explained, "I told Mary Lou not to bother taking down anything because I already told you about the clotheslines."

"Doesn't matter to me. In fact, I feel like I'm looking out my fourth floor bedroom window into the courtyard. I'm home," Bobby said with a smile.

Mary Lou and Billy were sitting at the kitchen table. Norma did the introductions.

"So, you're the Yankee that Norma likes so much," greeted Mary Lou with a big smile. Norma gave her a side-glance.

"That's me. Pleasure to meet you."

Bobby gave Mary Lou a little hug, which she was not expecting, and extended his hand to Billy. They shook and Billy gave Bobby a weak smile. "Nice to meet you."

Bobby nodded, "Yes, same here."

"What are you drinking, honey?" asked Norma.

"If you have scotch, fine. Beer will be okay, too. Thanks."

"We don't have scotch. Will bourbon do?"

"Yeah, why not?"

"Take off your coat and tie and relax," commanded Mary Lou. He did as he was told, and Mary Lou put them on a hanger. They sat around the table, talking small talk at first then started making plans for tomorrow's picnic. Bobby had nothing to add. They knew what to do, so he just observed.

Bobby was impressed with Mary Lou. She was tall and thin with a nice figure and blond hair. She had big blue eyes in a plain face with high cheekbones. She had a pleasant smile that seemed to never leave her face and a happy personality. Bobby could understand why Billy liked Mary Lou, but what did she see in him? He was about Norma's height, which meant he was nearly six inches shorter than Mary Lou. Billy had a potbelly and a small tattoo on each arm. They were visible because he sat there wearing only his undershirt and a pair of dirty dungarees. His sandy-colored hair was parted in the middle and made a sharp contrast with Bobby's crew cut. Mary Lou and Billy made a funny looking couple, but *C'est la vie*.

After a half-hour Mary Lou and Billy went into the living room to watch television. There was a clear space between the sofa, coffee table, and TV, which was about the only uncluttered area in the room. Norma and Bobby stayed in the kitchen.

"Do you mind if I change into my nightgown?"

"And deprive me of a very well-dressed, beautiful, young lady?"

"I promise to be very nice looking in my plain gown." She stood up.

Bobby gave her a long look, up and down, "You do look outstanding."

Norma sat on his lap, put her arms around his neck, and gave him the kiss she had wanted to at the beginning of the evening.

"I'll bring you some cold cream to wipe off the lipstick."

"It tastes good. Now, go get comfortable. I wish I could, but I don't think your roommates would like me walking around in my shorts."

"Billy wouldn't, but Mary Lou might. She likes you."

"How do you know? Did she slip you a note?"

"No, silly, the way she looked at you when you hugged her. She was charmed. When you were shaking hands with Billy, she looked at me and rolled her eyes up. Then she smiled and winked. That meant you were okay."

"Well, I think she's a very nice person. You're lucky to have a happy face, with a personality, around you."

Norma kissed Bobby on the cheek and left to change. He got up and walked around the kitchen, which was large enough to have all the necessities plus a big table with four chairs. It was very clean, except for the cigarette smoke in the air. There was a window facing the backyard. Bobby looked out. It was night, but the yard light attached to the house was on. He could see the garage, a barbeque area, a small swing set, and a sandbox. Just like the front yard, it was well kept.

Why, thought Bobby, *was he being so conscience of the condition of the house and kitchen?* He knew he was typecasting. That was terrible. There definitely was no cow dung on their shoes. Except for Billy. He was close to that image.

Bobby heard Norma talking to her roommates before she came back into the kitchen. She had on a modest, white cloth robe which was loosely tied and only slightly covering the front of her white, satin nightgown. She looked very nice, as she promised. Norma had a cold cream jar in one hand and a tissue in the other. She had removed her make-up, and she still looked good. Their eyes were locked and smiling. She wiped off the lipstick from the previous encounter.

Then Norma took the drink out of Bobby's hand, put it on the table and began to swallow his head, yet again. He loved it. After about a minute, she pulled away, took him by the hand, and as they walked past the living room, Norma yelled "Good night." They went down the hallway and entered her bedroom.

"Do you think we gave them the impression we were in a hurry?"

"Who cares?" said Norma with a big smile. "We're finally alone," and she closed the door.

Norma had her robe and nightgown off in a flash. Bobby unbuttoned his shirt while Norma worked on his pants. He never remembered getting undressed so fast. The bed was turned down, the top sheet folded over, and the pillows fluffed. He was looking for the mint on the pillows.

"Where are the mints?" Bobby joked.

Norma did not reply. Her eyelids were narrow, and her eyes intense. She was only thinking business. She pushed Bobby onto the bed and climbed on top of him.

CHAPTER VI
THE PICNIC

Bobby reached over to check the time. His wristwatch was on the night-stand. It was 7 A.M. Norma was on her left side, her face toward him. She was snoring very lightly, with her mouth opened slightly. It appeared she was in a deep sleep. It was amazing how much stamina she had with all the crazy hours she worked and with his being in her life for the last couple of days. But in a few days, he would be gone. That was something he didn't want to face: the good-bye. How was it going to go? What was going to be said? God, he had no idea. The affair had gone further than he expected. He wasn't sorry, but soon it would be time to pay the piper. That he was sorry about. Sometimes he wondered who was the country bumpkin. She was smart and knew how to handle her-self. She had completely controlled him last night after they left Fountain's. Bobby didn't mind. If Norma wanted to be boss, fine. He did-n't mind the penalty, and she extracted total pleasure.

He still didn't know much about her. All he knew was that she was a semi-nude dancer in a bar, she had grown up in Natchez, she had two sons, a mother and an aunt, she didn't finish high school, was twenty-one, 5'4" with brown eyes and brown hair, shapely, very pretty, and exceptionally beautiful when dressed as she was last night.

Bobby felt nature call and he found the bathroom. He looked in the mirror. The last few days were taking a toll on him. He now was even more amazed how good Norma always looked. He found Billy's shaving gear and figured he wouldn't mind if their house guest used it. Bobby saw their picture from Pete Fountain's displayed on her dresser, then he climbed back into bed.

Norma raised her head, looked at him with bleary eyes, and sank back into the pillow, "What time is it?"

"Seven forty-five."

"You smell like Billy does sometimes."

"I used his aftershave."

"You shaved?" She reached over to feel his face.

"Yes, and I washed up, too."

"Time for me to do the same." She got up, slipped on her robe, then turned and said. "I'm wearing this only because Billy's here," and winked.

Around ten A.M., Mary Lou and Billy got up and started moving about. Norma and Bobby soon followed. Billy wanted a regular breakfast but was shouted down by the girls. Since they would be going on a picnic, whatever coffee cake and bread was available would suffice for breakfast. Norma wore slacks and a blouse, and Mary Lou shorts and a tank top. Billy wore his dirty dungarees, but he did have on a clean T-shirt, and as for Bobby, his suit pants with a two-day-old white dress shirt.

"How far to the park?"

Norma replied, "About six blocks. There's a grocery store there on the corner where we can get our sandwiches, sodas, and beer. We'll bring blankets and pillows."

"Pillows? On a picnic?" questioned Bobby.

"That's Mississippi style," replied Norma with a smile.

On the way, Bobby decided some small talk was in order.

"Is that your landlord on the first floor?"

"No, they're renters as well. A nice family with two little girls. They let me use their phone. They're my emergency number. I sometimes bring the girls little toys and dolls to thank them for being so neighborly."

"Do they take care of the place?"

"Yes. Al cuts the grass, trims the bushes, and does patch-up work. When our sink or toilet backs-up, he's the one we call. His wife, Julie, bakes cakes and pies and will sometimes bring them by for us and the landlord."

"Well, he's doing a good job. I'm sure the landlord remembers it in the rent. By the way, what do you pay?"

"One hundred dollars a month. We could find a cheaper place, but the neighborhood is nice and safe, and it's good to be in a private house. Al and Julie watch out for us, and we do the same for them. After I called Mary Lou yesterday, she asked Al to check on how many were coming up. If there was more than two, he would have checked us out."

"How?"

"By talking to me. If I sounded strange—you know, like talking in a very high and shrill voice—he would know to call the police."

"And Mary Lou?"

"She would frown and speak in a low voice. That would tell him there is a problem. When we were walking up the stairs last night, he was watching us through the side window."

"Does your landlord know about the clotheslines?"

"Yes, he knows about them. The hooks were there when we moved in. We take down the lines when they're not being used, like for holidays or when the landlord comes at the first of the month, or when we have company. You're the exception."

"Hey, I'm honored to be considered part of the family, sharing in the clean laundry secrets."

She smiled at Bobby. "I'm sorry that Billy and Mary Lou started bickering in front of you. She said they would behave."

"Can anyone be nice with Billy?"

"I can't wait until he leaves. I gave him until the end of this month. He has about two weeks left."

"What about Mary Lou?"

"She agrees but is not public about it."

"Well, there's one thing they did together that impresses me."

"What's that?" Norma looked surprised.

"They're not smoking when we're with them. I could tell when I walked into your place there was smoke in the air, but they weren't smoking at the time."

"That's the one bad habit Mary Lou has."

"You mean besides Billy?"

"Yeah, Billy," Norma said as she shook her head.

"Well, at least they're not into reefers. You handle their smoking very well."

"I'm used to it. My daddy, momma, aunt, and brothers all smoke. Me and my sisters don't."

"Same with me. My dad smoked and my mother still does. So do most of my family and friends. You get used to it."

"Did your dad die because of smoking?"

"No, he got Hodgkin's cancer and suffered for two years, then died in 1957, on his birthday. Can you believe that?"

"When was he born?"

"June 21, 1909, and he died on June 21, 1957 when he turned forty-eight. It's also the first day of summer."

"And when were you born?" She smiled.

"You snuck that in very nicely. November 17, 1935."

"Guess what? We're both Scorpios. October 28, 1940."

"That explains a lot." Bobby smiled.

"Sure does," and Norma smiled even wider.

When they got to the grocery store, Bobby called Jerry while the others went to pick out the goodies. It was noontime.

"How's it going?" Bobby asked.

"Okay."

"Are you alone?"

"No."

"Listen, I'm going on a picnic with Norma and her roommates, Mary Lou and Billy Boy. I don't know about tonight."

"Neither do I."

"I'll call you around five. If you're not in, I'll leave a message."

"Okay. Talk to you later."

The way Jerry answered, in short statements, made Bobby believe Sandy was sitting right next to him, and she was probably not in a good mood.

When they got to the park, it was crowded with kids, kites, balls being tossed, and people eating and drinking. It was a big park. They eventually found a space with no activity and laid out the blankets. Norma made sure her blanket was at least ten feet from Mary Lou's: "No Smoking Zone."

Norma handed Bobby a ham and cheese sandwich and a beer. She had the ham and cheese with a soda. They ate in silence while listening to Mary Lou and Billy argue over the sandwiches, the cigarettes, and which music to listen to. Norma and Bobby looked at each other, smiled, and shrugged.

Bobby eventually laid back on his pillow. Norma pushed her pillow up against his and joined him, looking at the sky, which was blue and cloudless. There was a gentle breeze, and the temperature was in the low 80s with some humidity. Typical for the last five days.

Bobby was searching for what to say. Norma grabbed his hand and solved it for him.

"You want to know about me." It was a statement, not a question.

"Yes." *And about time*, Bobby thought.

"I grew up on small farm. I have three brothers and two sisters. I'm the youngest. My daddy left us five years ago. It was hard for my momma until her sister moved in after her husband died. My brothers and sisters are all married with children."

"Why did your father leave?"

"He got disgusted."

"About what?"

"It was a lot of things. The farm was hard work, and my momma nagged him about his drinking, and I disappointed him. I was his favorite."

"How?"

Norma looked directly at Bobby. "I got pregnant when I was fifteen. We got married because my momma said my son should have a daddy. I didn't love him. I named my baby after my daddy, Earl. It didn't matter to him, and when he left, it was for good."

"You said you have two sons."

This time she didn't look at Bobby. Her head was down. There was a strained silence. Norma was agonizing. Bobby was waiting.

Finally, she looked up. "Yes, but it wasn't with my husband. It was with his best friend, at the time."

Bobby was not expecting that. He was stunned. Norma kept talking.

"I didn't love my husband, but his friend and I always had fun. I did it on impulse. I thought he would marry me if I got divorced, but he didn't really care for me after all. I never saw him again. My husband left me, and we got a divorce. It was easy because I had an affair. I moved in with my momma and her sister. My boys are living with them."

Bobby looked at her, not believing how she could get things so screwed up. Knocked-up, fooled around, left with two kids from different men? This was not the Norma he knew, the sharp one. This was the country bumpkin from Natchez.

Norma looked at Bobby and could see he was confused. "You have to understand—living on a farm with my brother's friends and the neighborhood boys chasing me around since I was old enough to bleed."

"You telling me you were raped?"

Norma just sighed and shook her head. "No. The truth is, I enjoyed it."

"So, you're a nymph?"

"No, not that extreme, but I never hated it enough to turn it down either."

"Is that why you came to New Orleans?"

"No, it was to find work."

Bobby said nothing. His mind was in neutral. The only thing penetrating was the bickering between Mary Lou and Billy.

Norma grabbed his hand. She tried to smile, but it was weak. "My girlfriend worked here. She told me about the job. My momma and aunt said we needed the money, and I knew that."

"Why not work in Natchez?"

"They don't pay much. I'm not skilled, or trained, for a special job."

"Except?" said Bobby, sarcastically.

"You don't have to remind me, okay? I came here to have fun while making money, but then things changed."

"What changed?"

"I met Josephine."

Bobby was impressed. "What did she do for you?"

"She told me how lucky I was to have what she could never have."

"What was that?"

"Children and a family."

Bobby shrugged, as if to say, *What does that mean? So what?*

"You have to understand Josephine."

"I'm having trouble understanding you."

Norma continued, "She graduated from college, married a lawyer, had a nice home, but he left her because she couldn't have children. She came to New Orleans to get away from it all and have fun. My life seemed to parallel hers. I came here to have fun as well, but I have two boys, a momma, and an aunt, and I'm half her age. She has nothing. She would give anything to be in my shoes, to give birth and to have someone."

Norma stopped to catch her breath. She looked at Bobby. He was quietly listening.

"Then one night I got a call that Earl was very sick and in the hospital. I didn't know why. I didn't get home until the next night. All the way, on the bus, I worried. For the first time it occurred to me that, at anytime, my boys could be taken from me. Then I understood how empty Josephine felt and what she was trying to tell me. I stayed at home for two weeks. It was late January, and when I got back to New Orleans, I made changes. I started reading again, watched all the old movies I could on TV, and did not get involved with all the junk anymore."

"Do you mean your job?"

"Yes, that was the biggest change. I stopped doing some of the things that Mountain wanted me to do."

"Does that mean you stopped screwing?"

Norma glared at Bobby. "I couldn't just stop everything. I still needed my job until I worked my way out. Mountain got upset when I told him I would only do straight sex and jerking-off. No more blow jobs, doggie shows, and group acts."

"But, you still fucked?"

Norma just shook her head. "What did you expect from the girls when you came to New Orleans?"

Bobby sat in a long, stunned silence. Norma had her head in her hands.

Finally Bobby spoke. "I'm sorry, Norma. That was mean."

"No, you're right. It's time I stop everything and go home. I owe Mountain money and I'll pay him this week."

"Why do you owe him money?"

"Early on, I borrowed from future tip money to enjoy myself. I did things on impulse. Five months ago, when I told Mountain what I wasn't going to do, he got pissed-off. He increased his take on my tips. I was still able to send the same amount home since I wasn't wasting money anymore, but the money I have saved, I'll need to live on. I'll ask Josephine to loan it to me. She offered before, so now I'll take it."

"How much do you own him?"

"Four hundred dollars."

"Can I help you with that?"

"No, thank you. I don't want to be obligated."

"Josephine's money is all right, but mine is an obligation?"

"Yes. Let's not have a relationship based on me owing you money, okay?"

"Yeah, you're right." Bobby slowly nodded in agreement.

"Fine, that's settled then. I feel good that the decision was finally made." Norma kissed Bobby on the cheek.

He looked at her. "Congratulations. You're free."

"Not yet, but soon." She smiled and laid down on the blanket.

Mary Lou and Billy came over. "We're ready to leave. It's three o'clock."

"Go ahead," Norma replied. "We'll be home a little later. Take the leftovers and the radio. Thanks."

Bobby knelt next to Norma and gave her a big smile. "Josephine told me you don't take Mountain's shit anymore and that you're much wiser than two years ago. The other night, at the river, you told me you screwed up and were trying to get it back together. You have. You're not the same person you were in Natchez. You should be proud."

Norma sat up and put her arms around Bobby's neck. "Do you really mean that?"

"Of course. Don't you feel proud?"

"Very much. I feel relieved, too. I'm not afraid. I'm just going to do it. I'll call Josephine tonight and see when she'll have the money ready. If she can have it tomorrow, I'll tell Mountain that it's my last day."

"I'll be there tomorrow night to celebrate with you and Josephine, if she's there."

"She'll be there. I'll tell her to make it. She's important to me. So are you." They kissed lightly.

"Bobby, please believe me. What we shared the last two nights was because I care for you and not because I only wanted to satisfy myself."

"You said I would never believe what you were capable of if you loved someone. I found out."

"I showed it, but please don't ask me to say it. My track record is not very good on that subject."

They looked at each other, smiled, and nodded in agreement.

Bobby rolled up the blanket, put the pillows under their arms, and they started the walk back home.

"I know Earl's name. What's your other son's name?"

"Everett. He's three. Earl's five."

"Are they good boys?"

"They are very well behaved. My momma and aunt see to that."

"It must be rough on them without a man in the house."

"Thank goodness for my brothers. They live around town, near the kids. They treat them like their own. My sisters and their husbands are the same way. My boys get lots of attention, thank God."

"What was Earl's problem that got him into the hospital?"

"His appendix burst. It nearly killed him. He was in the hospital for a week. I stayed behind to nurse him for another week. It felt so good to see them at bedtime and kiss them goodnight. I can't wait until I'm with them again and my momma and aunt. I feel so sorry for Josephine, though. She doesn't know what she's missing."

"She does—that's why she was so concerned that you not miss out on it."

"You're right."

"You know, Norma, no matter how much Josephine preached about family, or how I made you feel good about yourself, it was still up to you to decide to make the change, and you did."

"Yes, and I'm so happy now."

They got to the grocery store at about 4:00.

"Norma, I'm going to call Jerry now. What do you want to do tonight? I don't know if we can go back to the motel."

"Was it used last night?"

"I don't know. I will never ask, and Jerry will never tell. We're funny that way. Like old time chivalry. The only way we can know is if we see the lady in bed, like the other morning."

"Well, I hope Jerry was as lucky as we were."

"What time do you go in tomorrow?"

"Ten."

"Listen, let's be sensible. We both could use a good night's sleep. I'll meet you and Josephine, and maybe Jerry, at nine tomorrow night, just before you quit. Hear that? Quit."

"Yes, yes, okay," she laughed. "You're right. I could sleep for days."

Bobby called Jerry and left a message that he'd be back that night. If that wasn't acceptable, leave the DO NOT DISTURB sign on the door. He'd make other plans.

"Jerry's not in. What if he wants the room tonight?"

"Then come back to my place, silly."

"Are you sure you want to give up your beauty sleep?"

Norma gave him a sly look. "When will you be leaving?"

"Early morning on Tuesday. We could stay for another day, if necessary."

"So tomorrow night will be our last night together?"

"Looks that way. Maybe Monday night if we leave Wednesday. No matter what, I'll get us a separate room. The place should be empty on Sunday and Monday nights. Okay?"

"Yes, I'd like that, being completely alone with you again."

Bobby began to feel the mixed emotions kicking in. Norma's were in full gear. She was wiping away tears.

"Listen, tomorrow or the next night may be the last for this trip. It doesn't mean it's the last time, period."

Norma smiled weakly. "Do you have a girlfriend?"

Bobby had wondered when that question would be asked and how he was going to answer it.

He looked at her with a shit-eating grin. "Well, I've been dating this girl, Lila, for two years. We grew up together on 5th Street."

"Is it serious?"

"Depends. Last Christmas I gave her an engagement ring and she refused it. It hurt. She was not sure but didn't say why, just no. I think it's because she's Italian with strong family values. Her last boyfriend wasn't Italian, like I'm not. I guess she doesn't want to go through that again."

"Does her family like you?"

"From all appearances, yes. They're always very nice and seem to accept me. The only times I feel uncomfortable are when they start talking in Italian and I can't understand them. It's my inferiority complex showing: I'm afraid they're talking about me. We still see each other, but anything serious is in limbo."

"Is she the only one?" asked Norma through narrowed eyelids.

"Except for you, yes."

"You know what I mean. Any other neighborhood girls, or otherwise?"

"There would have been another one, but she got married a couple years ago. Ellen was my first serious love. The one you remember the most. We were steady for nearly three years, starting from the time I was about sixteen. We lost touch after she started seeing Artie, and me, Lila."

"Okay, Valentino, once more. Any others?"

"Very funny, Movie Buff. Well, there is one phone call I have to make to satisfy Jerry."

"What does that mean?"

Bobby gave another shit-eating grin. "When we were at the motel in the Smokey Mountains, Jerry asked me about a girl I dated in college. I haven't seen her since 1956. I told Jerry she was probably married with kids. He challenged me to call her at her old work number, and if she was still there, and if she agreed, I'd make a date with her."

"Why is Jerry so anxious to see her again? And I'm assuming she's still there, single, and willing to date you."

"Jerry, John, Fats, Danny, Ray, Charlie, Eddie, and all the other guys and girls from the Lamplighter's, liked Joan. She had a personality like Mary Lou's, made everyone feel good when she was around. That's why she got her nickname, Bubbles."

"Bubbles? You're kidding? She must be from Bourbon Street," Norma laughed.

"No, she's not. She's just that, a bubbly person. I'll make that call and that issue will be settled. She's not there, not after six years."

Norma looked at Bobby, gave him a sly smile, and slowly shook her head.

They arrived at Norma's house. "I'll go upstairs and pick up my jacket, tie, and photo, and say *adieu* to Mary Lou and Billy."

"How about having one of the leftover sandwiches for dinner?"

"Sounds good to me. I'm hungry."

Norma put her pillow down and her arms around Bobby's waist. "Can you stay for a few hours? Not all night, just till eight or so?"

"Of course. That will make me very happy."

"No, that will make us very happy," corrected Norma.

Before going upstairs, Norma took Bobby to her neighbors' place, where she made a call to Josephine while Bobby watched the evening news on the family's TV with Al and Julie, a very pleasant couple, and their daughters, Joann and Diann, both very cute and shy. They had just finished their dinner.

Norma called for Bobby to get to the phone, which was in the kitchen, next to the living room. "Josephine wants to talk to you." She left the room with a big smile.

"Hello there, Sapphire, it's me, Andy," joked Bobby.

"I never knew when I met you that I'd have an ally, but I should have guessed with all the attention and gift giving you were doing," said Josephine, ecstatically.

"Yep. We were both on the same wavelength and didn't know it. You wouldn't believe how it all unfolded. I told Norma no matter how much you preached or I encouraged her, it had to be her decision."

"She will be so much happier back with her family because she'll remember her experience in New Orleans, the good and the bad."

"Well, let's not count on it yet. She has a way to go."

"I told her I would give her the money tomorrow, so don't you worry about that, honey. By the way, I didn't get your gift yet, but she just told me about your date last night and that you were really impressed with her outfit, especially her pearls."

"I did say they were elegant. And she was absolutely beautiful. I still can't believe it."

"That's because you still see her as a barroom dancer—and a Southern one, to boot."

"Yeah, yeah, I know. Cultural differences."

Josephine laughed. "Now, I recently saw this single pearl on a gold chain with matching earrings. Very nice, simple, delicate, and it was on sale for twenty dollars."

"Sounds good to me. I'll trust you on that. Get it and I'll pay you tomorrow night. You will be there, right?"

"I wouldn't miss it for the world. Just to see Mountain's face. He thought he had her all locked up."

"Remind me to give you my address and phone number for future use." Just then, Norma walked in the room. "Well, here's the Girl Wonder. See you tomorrow, and thanks. Good night."

Bobby waited while Norma made her last few comments and hung up.

She cradled Bobby's face in her hands and gently kissed him.

"Don't say anything, Norma. You don't have to."

Norma nodded, smiled and kissed him again.

They went back to the living room and said their good-byes. Al said, "Be nice to see you again."

"One never knows," replied Bobby.

They walked out the side door and climbed the steps to Norma's.

When it was time to leave, Norma gave Bobby one of her dynamite kisses. "Thank you," sighed Norma.

"Don't say that," whispered Bobby with a smile. "Lovers don't have to say 'thank you'."

"Did you just make that up, Valentino?" mused Norma.

"No, I'm not that romantic. Ellen said that to me," confessed Bobby. "See you tomorrow night, and get a good night's rest."

"You bet, on both counts. Got everything?"

"Uh- huh. Especially our picture."

"Don't you ever lose it!" glared Norma.

"Yes, Mother," replied Bobby with a smile.

Norma gave Bobby a kiss on the cheek, "Good night, honey."

He walked a few blocks to a candy store and called a cab.

CHAPTER VII
THE BEATING

Bobby arrived at the motel about 9 P.M. Jerry was alone watching Sid and Imogene on TV. There would be no going back to Norma's tonight.

"Hello there. Where's Sandy?"

"She's out with Mary Jane."

"Weren't you invited?"

"I didn't want to go. Sandy's okay, but she complained once too much about Mary Jane being alone, so I told her to go out with her girl-friend tonight."

"Was Sandy with you when I called at noon?"

"Sandy and Mary Jane were here, and I didn't want to talk too much. Tensions were high."

"I guessed by your monosyllable answers. Did you have dinner?"

"Yes, I did, but let's go for coffee and dessert and talk about what's been going on."

After they got seated and ordered, Jerry looked at Bobby. "So, how did you enjoy the picnic?"

"Before I get to that, let me start with the apartment. It's on the 2nd floor of a private house. The first thing that strikes you are the clotheslines in the living room and kitchen. It's like you're looking out your window into the backyard."

"Did they have clothes on them?"

"Yeah. The one thing about them is that they are clean conscience. Except for Billy, Mary Lou's boyfriend, who's mooching off them until he finds a job, which he hasn't tried to do. Norma gave him until the end of the month to clean up his act."

"Other than lazy, how does he act? What does he look like?"

"Short and dumpy. No hard feelings, Jerry, but you at least have a build. He's also crummy looking and acts like a jerk. Straight out of Tennessee Williams. I was waiting for him to start yelling, 'Stella, Stella!'"

That broke Jerry up, "That says it all. How's Mary Lou?"

"She's been Norma's girlfriend since childhood. They get along real well. Mary Lou's tall and lanky with a healthy pair of lungs and a nice figure. She has a plain face, but it's likeable. The main thing about her is her personality. It never quits. Always makes you feel good. She's like Bubbles."

"Speaking of whom, you will call her when you get back home, right?"

"Right, but she's not there anymore. Believe me."

"What does Mary Lou see in Billy?"

"I don't know. They've been going together for years. Maybe she's just comfortable and doesn't want to chance it out there, single and alone. They're always fighting over the dumbest things. That's about the only time you see Mary Lou being testy. But with a character like Billy, that's easy."

"He probably has a twelve-inch long schlunge."

"Yeah, and two inches across. For all I know, that could be the answer."

"Tell me about the picnic. Was it like *The Movie*?"

"We didn't dance, but there were sparks flying. It started off slowly, then the conversation picked up steam. Eventually I got to know just about everything there is to know about Norma."

"Is that good or bad?"

"A mix, but mostly good. The main thing is she decided to quit and go back home to her kids, her mother, and her aunt."

"She has children?"

"Yeah, two boys, five and three. She's divorced." No need to go into the gory details at this time, Bobby reasoned.

"When will she quit?"

"Tomorrow, after she gets the money from Josephine that she owes Mountain."

"Why does she owe him?"

"In her early days, she ran around a lot, was wild, and drew on her future tip money."

"How much?"

"Four hundred."

"That much. Does she smoke joints?"

"No, she doesn't smoke, so I doubt she's into reefers. Drinking mostly."

"Does being 'wild' mean she's really into sex?" Jerry asked with a shrug.

"No. She admits she didn't always refuse it, but she doesn't breathe heavy and go sniffing after it either."

"Since she calmed down, what occupies her free time?"

"She's back to reading books and watching old movies on TV."

"What kind?"

"Romantic comedies. She likes the give and take, Tracy and Hepburn style."

"She has a sharp tongue and a good sense of humor, I'll grant her that. And, she's also good looking." Jerry smiled.

"Anything more you want to know, Question Man?"

"No. I just hope she quits tomorrow."

"I was thinking of inviting her to New York for a couple of weeks."

"Are you nuts? Where's she going to stay, on Avenue B? What about Lila? What's Norma going to do while you're at work?"

"I'm thinking of this like a reward for leaving New Orleans," mused Bobby, not acknowledging any of Jerry's questions.

"It may be more like a cruel joke when she gets back to Mississippi," Jerry replied in cold logic.

Bobby thought for a while. "Yeah, you're right. I just wanted to do something."

"Like maybe marry her? That really would be stupid."

"You sound like Josephine."

"That's because we're the only sensible ones around," Jerry gloated.

"Are you going to join us for tomorrow night's celebration?"

"Maybe. Depends on what Sandy wants to do."

"When do they leave?"

"Monday afternoon."

"Are we still set for Tuesday or can we move it to Wednesday?" Bobby asked.

"Whatever you want to do. You're the one involved. I don't want you bitching about me breaking up a budding romance," joked Jerry.

"What did you do yesterday?"

"The pool in the morning with Sandy and Mary Jane. Met some more of our neighbors, then lunch and a movie with Sandy. That's when she started complaining again about Mary Jane being alone. So now they're together."

"What movie?" asked Bobby to get Jerry's mind off the Sandy situation.

While Jerry was talking about the movie, Bobby was only half-listening, thinking mostly about tomorrow night with Norma. They got back to their room around eleven.

At breakfast Bobby inquired about the nearest church but never went. Too lazy, or just too guilty? They were lounging at the pool when Sandy and M.J. arrived. Bobby was surprised there was no animosity showing. Sandy went into the pool with Jerry. Bobby knew he owed Jerry one, so he decided to pay him back.

"Would you like to see the movie that they saw yesterday?" Bobby asked.

"No, thank you. I have other plans," replied Mary Jane with a smile that said "Shove it!"

Hey, great, thought Bobby. *Now, no worry on what to say about this evening.*

Later, a guest arrived who knew Sandy and Mary Jane. He introduced himself to Jerry and Bobby and started to carry on a conversation with Mary Jane.

So that's her date, thought Bobby.

"Looks like M.J.'s spoken for," Bobby said to Jerry as they went for a bite to eat.

"Yeah, and Sandy wants to spend the day with me alone."

"All's well that ends well," quoted Bobby. "After lunch I just want to take it easy. Make some calls to Lila and Maggie."

"What can you possibly tell them about your trip? You got beat up in Memphis and screwed in New Orleans! You better hope they're not home."

Bobby agreed. "It will take some imagination."

"Imagination, my ass. You'll have to lie, big time. Like 'Norma who'?"

Speaking about Norma, Bobby wondered how it was going down with Mountain. Whatever! As long as Josephine had the money and Norma the nerve.

After lunch Bobby went to his room and called his mother and his girlfriend. He spoke in generalities about the weather, the people, the food, the entertainment, the motel, and, of course, that he couldn't wait to get home. He then turned in to take a nap.

Bobby was awakened by Jerry getting dressed. It was six P.M.

"I'm going to dinner with Sandy. You want to join us?"

Bobby knew Jerry was just being polite. "No, thanks. I'll be getting up soon and grab something at the restaurant before I go to the club. You two are welcome to come by for a celebration drink later."

"I doubt we'll make it. Send her our best wishes."

Bobby arrived at Paree a little after nine P.M. The audience chairs were filled and there were six sailors in attendance. He noticed because there was a sea of white uniforms in the front row. He looked for Josephine but couldn't find her. He figured she was running late but would be showing up shortly. He looked for Norma, but she couldn't be seen, either. He found a spot at the bar in front of the audience and ordered a scotch and water from Ed, who had a smirk on his face, probably because Bobby ordered a mixed drink.

Halfway through his drink, Norma appeared at his side and put her left hand on his right arm.

Bobby looked at her and was startled. Her eyes were red and puffy from crying.

"What's the matter? What happened?" he blurted out.

"It didn't go too well with Mountain. He's going to make it hard for me to leave."

"What happened?"

"I gave him the four hundred, but he claims I owe him more money than I do."

"How much more?"

"Four hundred more."

"That's double!"

"He says it's due to interest, and he's going to hassle me until it's paid off, even if it means having me arrested and taken to court."

"He can't do that," Bobby said, but he knew what Mountain could do: jerk around the interest rate and scare her so the loan could never be paid off unless he said so.

Bobby turned to Norma. She was looking at him in her daze. He was about to tell her not to worry about it when a huge, fat body came between them.

"Get back to work," he growled at Norma.

"Wait a minute, I'm talking to her."

Bobby no sooner finished his sentence when Mountain turned and swung with his right fist. It caught Bobby flush on his left eyebrow, and he fell off the bar stool while his left hand desperately held onto the bar rail. Mountain continued swinging at Bobby's inclined body. Bobby was trying to block the shots with his right hand but was not doing too good a job: He got nailed a couple more times. He knew he couldn't hit the ground because Mountain hated him so much, he would probably stump him into oblivion. Next thing Bobby saw was a flood of white uniforms. The six sailors left their seats. Four were ganging up on Mountain, and two were leaning over Bobby to help him to his feet.

"Man, you're a mess. Better get out of here."

"Why did he attack you?" asked the other one.

Bobby shrugged and looked in the mirror behind the bar. He could see the blood coming out of this left eyebrow. He looked at the dancer, who was not moving; her hands covered her mouth, and a shocked look was on her face as she watched the action, which was now about thirty seconds old. He looked down, and his white shirt was covered with blood. He looked around for Norma and couldn't find her. He looked at the sailors who had helped him, nodded, and said, "Thank you, and thank your crew." The fighting sailor pals were still banging away at Mountain and some of his friends as Bobby left the bar.

When he walked into the street, he got gasps from passersby. He realized he had to clean himself up. He headed toward The Famous

Door and right into the men's room. When he entered, there were a few of the musicians ready to leave. He had met them before.

"What happened to you?" one asked.

"Mountain was beating me up and some sailors broke it up," Bobby replied as if they could understand him.

"Start washing up."

"Take your shirt off. I have a spare one you can wear," said another.

"The first thing to do is to stop that bleeding," said the third wisely.

Thanks to helping hands, Bobby was cleaned up and dressed in a clean shirt. His dark blue dress pants didn't show blood, just a dark stain.

Bobby was given a clean hand towel to act as a pressure bandage to his cut. The only way to stop the flow was to keep pressure on the wound. He threw his undershirt in the trash bin and left his bloody shirt on the floor, under the sink, in the corner. One of the musicians was going to take care of it, the one who gave Bobby a clean shirt.

Bobby thanked them profusely and shook their hands. "You and the sailors are my guardian angels tonight. I can't thank you guys enough."

"Stay away from that joint."

"Come here to friendly people."

"And to enjoy great music!"

Bobby walked through the place with his left hand over his left eye. Without the bloody shirt, he didn't draw any unusual attention. He just looked like a guy nursing a hangover.

Bobby walked down the sidewalk away from the Door and the Club. He wondered what was happening at Paree. How did the sailors end the battle? What was going through Norma's head as she watched Bobby get clobbered? He then remembered they had planned a last night at the river, so he headed in that direction. It was nearly 10:30. He was hoping she would be there waiting for him. Bobby arrived at the dock, and he was alone. He began to think various scenarios. What if the fight turned into a real brawl and Norma got involved and got arrested with the rest of them? Not likely. If Mountain only got arrested with the sailors, then Norma would be free to leave. Since she wasn't here, that didn't happen. What was keeping her? Bobby was sorry he didn't get Josephine's phone number. She would have all the answers.

Bobby started to leave at midnight, but decided to give her more time. Finally, at one A.M., he realized it was too late for her to show up. He walked, looking for a cab. He came to the church at the waterfront, but it was locked.

Town and Country, please. It's over at...."

"I know the place," said the cabby, looking at Bobby, whose hand was holding a bloody towel over his eye. "What happened to you?"

47

"I got into a fight with a bartender on Bourbon Street," Bobby lied a little.

"What about? The tab?"

"No. To be honest, it was over one of the girls. He didn't like the fact she was attracted to me."

"Hey, that happened to me about ten years ago. The bouncer worked me over because Dolly liked me more than him."

"So what happened?"

"I never saw Dolly again, but my five brothers and a bunch of friends went back and wrecked the place."

"It's nice that this is your hometown, and you have family and friends here. I'm fifteen hundred miles away from New York with only my buddy, Jerry, who wasn't with me tonight."

"Well, don't say that you don't have friends in high places."

"What does that mean?"

"Don't get smart. You're staying at the Town and Country, right? It's mob owned, and don't tell me you didn't know."

So, that's why Josephine was so impressed about us staying at that motel, thanks to a friend's recommendation. "A very, very, good friend," as she had stressed it. Some cabbies, and street-smart people, would know who controls what. Sometimes it's common knowledge. Thanks to the press, anyone who cares knows where the wiseguys eat on Mulberry Street. This was a cab driver who paid attention to what he read, saw, and heard.

"Yeah, the place was recommended to me by a very, very close friend. I guess I could complain to the management about my treatment as a law-abiding guest in their fair city."

"I'm sure they'll notice," he smiled.

Bobby thanked him, paid him, and he drove away. Bobby looked at the restaurant and wondered what to do. Finally, he decided. What the hell! All that could happen, worse than the beating, was that they would all laugh at him. Emotional embarrassment was sometimes more painful than physical damage. With that in mind he walked into the place, not knowing exactly what he was going to say. He would just have to wing it.

CHAPTER VIII
THE MAN

Bobby walked in. There was one waitress behind the counter where there was only one person seated. The other waitress was at a table occupied by two customers. "The Table" in the back was occupied, as usual, with men smoking and drinking. They were businessmen of another stripe. The man sitting at the counter looked at Bobby and turned away. The waitress came over.

"Are you okay?" She recognized Bobby as one of the guests she had served over the last six days.

"I'm hurting a little—mostly my pride, believe it or not. Thanks for asking." She nodded, and Bobby continued. "You can do me a favor and please ask one of the gentlemen at that table to come over and see me."

She looked at Bobby quizzically. "Okay. Why don't you sit in the booth over there," she pointed and then handed Bobby a menu.

Bobby watched as she went to "The Table," to one man in particular. He was "The Man." She bent over to talk to him. Her conversation was punctuated by her bobbling head as she told him about one of the guests, the one with a bloody face, who wanted to speak to him. His head was down as she spoke into his ear. When she finished, she straightened up, and "The Man" looked in Bobby's direction. He then stood up, said something to the waitress, and they headed toward Bobby.

When they got to the booth, Bobby stood up and stuck his hand out to "The Man." "Hello, my name is Bobby. Thank you for coming over to talk to me."

"The Man" shook his hand. "Call me John." He looked a little like George Raft.

He turned to the waitress, "Helen, please bring an ice pack, a wet towel, a dry one, and a cup of black coffee. You want anything, Bobby?"

49

"Yes, coffee with cream, please."
Helen left and they sat down.

John stared at Bobby, and he had a little smile on his face.

Bobby blurted out. "Listen, John, a family member who lives on 13th Street and 2nd Avenue and knows the Rocky Graziano's very well, told me to stay at the Town and Country when I told him about my trip here to New Orleans. Uncle Jimmy said to call him if I had any problems. If that wasn't possible, then go to the management and tell them what happened."

"So, what happened?" replied John, who looked unimpressed.

"Well, I was at the Club Paree last night talking to one of the girls when Mountain came over and started to beat me up."

That got John's attention. "So, you're the one who caused the problem."

Now, it was Bobby's turn to be surprised. "Caused the problem? Bullshit! He hit me with a blind-side shot and continued to belt me. If it wasn't for the sailors, he would have killed me." Bobby shook his head in disbelief while John stared at him.

Helen arrived with the ice pack and towels. Another waitress brought the coffee and left. Helen took away the bloody hand towel Bobby had held for nearly four hours. Some of the dried blood was pulled away from the eyebrow, and the earlier excessive blood flow was now a trickle.

"How bad is it?" Bobby inquired.

"I can't tell because it's in the eyebrow. It looks like an inch at least." She dabbed around the cut, and the face, with the wet towel to remove as much dried blood and stain as possible without the benefit of soap and hot water. She avoided the cut area. She wrapped the dry towel around the ice pack, placed it in Bobby's left hand and directed it over the wound. She had done this before. "The swelling should go down," she advised.

"Thank you," replied Bobby.

John nodded his head in an approving manner, and Helen left.

"You don't believe me, do you?" asked Bobby.

"Why did the sailors get involved?"

"I was at the bar between the dancers and where they were sitting. They saw me talking to this girl when Mountain came over, interrupted our conversation, and then attacked me. Two of them helped me up while the other four kept Mountain away from me." Bobby stopped and shook his head. "Mountain was so pissed at me, he continued swinging, and the sailors just fought back. They told me I was a mess and to get the hell out of there, so I did."

"You didn't know them at all?"

"I've never met them before tonight."

50

Bobby looked down and began to put things together. *Mountain told his bosses the fight started because a troublemaker, with Navy friends, was harassing one of his girls.*

"Wait a minute, John. I know what you're thinking, but please don't believe that fat bastard. He's bad for business—beating up a customer and fighting with others."

"He might not be too bright, but he has to protect his girls."

"But I wasn't harassing the girl."

Bobby thought for a moment and decided to lay it all out. "All right. Let me give you all the details. My buddy Jerry and I went to Paree when we hit town. I met one of the girls and bought her a drink. We enjoyed each other's company so much that we went out a few times. My presence didn't affect her work. She was always hustling, ordered the Special whenever she could." Not true. Bobby looked down. He had to build a case for Norma. Mountain's credibility was in doubt. Ed had the reputation of being too greedy, always complaining that the customers were not drinking enough. Charlie was the unknown. Because of his dislike for Mountain and Ed, he just might shade the truth in Norma's favor, if it went that far.

"How serious are you?"

"I got to know she's from Mississippi, been here for two years, divorced with two small boys who now live with her mother and aunt on a small farm in Natchez. I know she sends money home every week."

"They all do, or so they say," smirked John.

Bobby looked at him, wondering how much he believed and if he was really concerned about knowing the truth. Bobby continued to explain. "The problem was she decided to quit and go back home. It started six months ago, after Christmas, when her younger son nearly died because of a burst appendix. She realized how much she missed them. Before she quit, she had to pay back Mountain the money she borrowed. She had been saving—"

John interrupted. "Did you give her the money?"

"No. She had it saved and was waiting for the right time to tell Mountain."

"Why was now the right time?"

"Because I convinced her that she belonged back in Natchez, raising her kids and being with her family."

"And you're surprised Mountain hit you? You're taking away his business." John glared at Bobby.

And taking away your business as well, Bobby thought. "She's not right for this work. She's a country girl from a farm. The big city is too much for her."

Bobby floundered for the words, the reason she's not good for business. "She's an unhappy employee. Mountain treats her like he owns her, his property. He told her she couldn't leave because she owed him twice the amount of money due to interest. He also told her if she didn't pay up, he'd have her thrown in jail. Until then, she worked for him, period. The last thing she said to me, before all hell broke loose, was that she felt like she was a slave."

At that, John's eyebrows rose a little. Bobby knew he hit the right word, the reason. He looked at John. "Nobody likes to work if they feel they're in servitude."

Helen came over with two cups of fresh coffee. Bobby looked at her. She did not return his gaze. She was very businesslike, very efficient. She knew who was the boss. John nodded, and she smiled and left.

John was silent for a while and then asked, "What's her name?"

"Norma."

"How much does she owe?"

"It was four hundred dollars until Mountain doubled it. All she had to give him was four hundred dollars. She was upset and crying when we talked about it. Then Mountain got between us, yelled at Norma to get back to work, and started beating me up. That's what the sailors saw."

John started nodding, and it appeared he was in deep thought.

Bobby realized it was time to end the facade. "John. I have to be honest. I really do a have a very good friend, Jimmy, but he is not my uncle, and he didn't tell me to stay here. It was picked by pure choice. Tonight, the cab driver told me about this place's connections." Bobby just stared at John and waited for an explosion.

"And I suppose all the rest was made-up as well?"

"No. It was the truth. That's why I had to own up to the bullshit I first told you. I thought the worst that could happen was that you'd laugh at me."

"That's not the worst. We could get very annoyed at the deception."

"Oh shit! I never though of that."

"Weren't you worried that I would ask for Uncle Jimmy's number and call him?"

"I never thought of that either."

"You didn't plan very well, did you?"

"Obviously not. I had a ten second discussion with myself before I came in here. My decision was pure emotion. I'm just so fucking frustrated about what happened—not just my beating. It's because Norma's dream was shattered. Not being able to go home and having to be tied down to that fat bastard." Bobby shook his head in disbelief. It all came tumbling down, all the talk and the hope.

He looked up at John, who had his hands cupped around his chin and was looking very intently at Bobby.

Finally his hands came down, and he gave Bobby one of those shit-eating grins. "I have to hand it to you, you do have moxie."

"Well, I don't know about that. If I had thought for another ten seconds, I probably would have gone back to the room and started packing."

John chuckled. "Well, let me tell you, sonny, your sincerity has saved you."

Bobby looked at him with eyes wide open, in disbelief. "Thank you, John. Thank you so much."

"When are you leaving?"

"Day after tomorrow, or Wednesday."

"Don't go back to the bar."

"I was hoping to see Norma again."

"Get a message to her to come and stay here with you tonight. I'll tell the manager to get you a room."

"Thanks."

"And, we don't want you walking around town. Keep a low profile."

"Okay. I don't know what else to say, John."

"Right now, just do what I'm telling you to do. Did you tell anyone what happened to you?"

"Only the cabdriver. I told him I had a fight with a bartender because of a girl."

"You didn't mention what bar?"

"No."

"Okay. Lucky you didn't go to a hospital."

"Why's that?"

"We have a new district attorney, Jim Garrison, who ran on a get-tough-on-crime campaign to get the votes. He wants all doctors and hospitals to report severe beatings like they report gun wounds."

"What's a severe beating?"

"Anyone badly bruised, many cuts, and any wound that requires stitches."

"What if it's an accident?"

"The police investigation will determine whether it was an accident or not."

"What about the cabby? What if he decides to become a good citizen and report this incident?"

"Well, if he did, the police would have been here by now. He won't say anything."

John took out a pen, wrote something on a napkin, and handed it to Bobby. "Here, call this number at eight A.M. confirming your 8:30 doctor's appointment and get directions to his office. Then call a taxi to pick you up at the Pantry House across the street."

"Do I have to tell him anything?"

"No. It doesn't matter."

Bobby knew what that meant: It wouldn't be reported. "Thank you, again."

"Just take it easy tomorrow. When the shock wears off, you'll feel the aches and pains. You have some bruises on your face, which will hurt. When the painkillers wear off, after the stitches, the fun will really begin."

"I'll need Norma for some tender loving care. By the way, what's she to tell Mountain about not showing up for work?"

"Nothing. Norma doesn't work for him anymore."

It took a few seconds for Bobby to comprehend what John said. When it did, he jumped up. "My God, she's free!" he yelled. "John, I could kiss you."

"You do that and you'll really be in trouble. Sit and calm down."

Bobby did what he was told, but he was still shaking out of excitement. He couldn't believe it was all over. Norma could go home.

"I'll ask you again. How serious are you about Norma?"

"It's mixed emotions. She's smart, has a sense of humor, cares about her family. She admits to sometimes acting on impulse, which isn't always good. My friends, Jerry and Josephine, tell me I'm crazy to continue the relationship, but I'm having trouble controlling my feelings."

"Who's Josephine?"

"I met her at the bar. She knows all the players. She's a regular there."

John nodded his head as if to say, *"Yeah, I know her."*

"Well, they're right. When you leave town, leave everything behind. It was fun, bitter-sweet, but it's time to let it go." John said that with a glare at Bobby.

"I understand," Bobby said reluctantly.

John got up, and so did Bobby. "Thank you, again. We owe you so much. I can't wait to tell Norma. She'll go crazy."

"I hope not. You take care of yourself, and don't do anything stupid."

Bobby nodded and they shook hands. John walked to the counter, spoke with Helen and then went back to "The Table."

Bobby finished his coffee. He couldn't believe how good he felt. He walked to the counter register. Helen came over. "Do I owe you anything?"

She shook her head, no. "It sounds like you did a little celebrating over there," she said with a smile.

"Yeah, John told me some good news, and I jumped up in joy."

"Makes you forget about your aches and pains, doesn't it? I left a message for the manager to get you a room for tonight and maybe tomorrow night, Mr. and Mrs. Smith."

"Sounds good, very original. And, I thank you, Helen, for your nursing skills." Bobby smiled and gave her a ten dollar bill.

"That's very generous, and I thank you."

"Well, you and your staff have been very helpful." He nodded in the direction of "The Table."

"Yeah, my staff, right on!" she laughed.

As Bobby walked to the room, he realized what word caught John's attention and the reason why he let Norma go home. The word was "servitude" and the reason was that he didn't want D.A. Garrison to hear about Norma's situation. "Break up the slave girl racket on Bourbon Street" would make a great law and order issue for the newly elected district attorney. John didn't need that publicity, no matter if it only applied to Norma. Maybe it didn't. Maybe there was more of it. Whatever, John had Mountain to thank for bringing it up with Norma, who mentioned it to Bobby, who told John. Norma had probably told Josephine, and anyone else who wanted to know, why she was crying. After the publicity and investigation, indictments could follow. John definitely didn't want any of that. Bobby believed that John and his organization did not condone Mountain's method of possession. There always would be a supply of girls who wanted to bar-dance for the pleasure, the money, the excitement, whatever. Nobody had to force them. They definitely did not have to enslave them. Only Mountain would for his personal pleasure.

Unfortunately for Mountain, his goal was not in the best interest of the overall business. Bobby wondered how John was going to handle the situation with Mountain. He wished he could be that fly on the wall. Mountain is not only "not that bright," according to "The Man," but now he was a complete liability. Mountain did not have much of a future. All Bobby could think was, *good riddance.*

Bobby's thoughts now turned to Norma. He wished he had Norma's neighbor Al's phone number to call her. He also wished he had Josephine's home number. He would try and reach Josephine at the Paree.

Bobby tried to be quiet after he entered the motel room and started undressing, but Jerry woke up. Bobby kept his back to him.

"What time is it?"

"A little after three."

"How did it go?"

"Early in the evening, it was a disaster. But lately, it's been a great success."

"What do you mean?"

Bobby turned around. Jerry was startled at what he saw. "What the fuck happened to you?"

"Mountain sucker-punched me."

Jerry jumped out of bed. "Let's get dressed and pay a visit to that bastard." Jerry was very upset.

"Jerry, Jerry, relax. He's going to get his, in spades."

Bobby sat Jerry down and told him the whole story, from the discussion with Norma, to the hit by Mountain, the sailors' involvement, the help at The Famous Door, the wait at the waterfront, the cab ride, and finally, the meeting with "The Man." All of it.

"You actually walked in there to talk to them? What balls!"

"John called it moxie."

"And you told him you were connected?"

"No, not me, but my very good friend, 'Uncle Jimmy.'"

"And then you told him the truth?"

"That's what saved me. John understood how I felt, what Norma was going through, and how bad Mountain is for business with the 'slave' issue."

"Well," Jerry smiled, "it would be interesting to find out what happens to him."

"Right now I'm more interested in finding out how Norma is doing. After the doctor's visit, I'll try calling the club for Josephine."

Jerry volunteered, "I can go down there and look for her and Norma, if she's working early."

"No, don't go near that place. They know we're friends. John wants us to stay away. Maybe he wants Mountain to believe he scared us off and get him to relax and maybe do another stupid thing."

Bobby began to feel real tired. His head began to throb. He went for the aspirins. "I'd better lay down." He fell asleep as soon as his head hit the pillow.

Jerry woke him up at 7:45. "Time to make that call to the doctor."

Bobby got dressed, and at eight A.M. he called and got directions. He then called for a cab and waited for it in front of the Pantry House. He and got to the doctor's office at 8:30. It was a short ride, three miles at the most.

The sign said GENERAL MEDICAL GROUP, OFFICE HOURS 9 AM TO 5 PM, MONDAY THRU FRIDAY. The front door was unlocked, and the doctor was waiting for him in the reception room. They shook hands, and Bobby was lead into his office. Bobby sat on the examining table, and the doctor examined the wound. After giving Bobby a local anesthetic, he shaved off the left eyebrow. The doctor cleaned the area with a cotton ball soaked in alcohol and began stitching the cut. He handed Bobby a mirror so he could see the results. The scar was a little more than one inch long. It followed the line of his eyebrow, along the ridge of his eye socket.

"You will never see the scar after the eyebrow grows back." He handed Bobby a bottle of painkillers. "Take one every couple hours as you need them for the pain, but never more than six in one day." He then handed Bobby a box. "It's special bandages for that type of wound over an eye. Change two times a day after you clean the area with alcohol."

"I'll have to get that."

"No, I'll give you a bottle along with a box of cotton balls. Now watch how I apply the bandage."

When he was finished, he shook Bobby's hand.

"Thank you, Doc. How much do I owe you?"

"Nothing. Your bill has been paid. One thing to remember though: if you have constant pain after taking two pills, call me. I'll have to see you again."

"Infection?"

"Yes. It sometimes happens, but not to worry. It can be treated."

"Thanks, again."

Bobby could hear someone in the reception room. It was 9:15.

"That's my receptionist. You can leave through that door. It leads directly to the hallway. You can catch a taxi at the hotel across the street. Good-bye."

Bobby got back to the motel about 9:45.

"That was fast."

"He was waiting for me. He had the shot, the razor, the needle, and thread ready to sew."

"Did he ask you any questions?"

"No, nothing. In fact, he told me the bill was paid. You, me, John, and the doctor are the only ones who know I got stitches from an accident that never happened. 'What beating?' That's the reason John doesn't want me walking around sporting a bandage."

Jerry looked at the bandage. "When you change bandages, let me see the stitches. I'll compare it to the work my dad does." Jerry's father was a doctor, Bobby's doctor, in fact, and the first person Bobby would see when they got back to New York.

"Oh, Josephine called," Jerry said with a smile.

"And you waited so long to tell me?"

"I wanted to hear about your operation."

"What did she say?" Bobby asked eagerly.

"She found out what happened to you and was concerned."

"Did she way anything about Norma?"

"Norma's okay. She'll tell you when she calls back around 10:15."

"Thank God, she's all right."

Bobby laid down. The anesthetic was starting to wear off. It would be pain pill time soon.

"Hey, Jerry, check the pain pills I got. You're a pharmacist. Do they look okay?"

Jerry looked at the pills. Mumbled some medical words. The only one Bobby recognized was "morphine."

"Yes, they're standard. No problem, unless you're allergic, which I doubt. My dad probably gave you a prescription for them in the past."

Bobby wasn't listening. He was basking in the knowledge that Norma was okay and was now free to go home.

Finally the phone rang.

"Hello."

"Bobby, it's Josephine. How are you? We've been so worried."

"I'm fine now. The cut over the eye bled easily, so there was more blood than pain. I got some bruises but nothing big. What's up with Norma? How's she doing?"

"She saw you get hit, and she couldn't watch. She turned and walked away crying, from what the other girls told me. Mountain took a beating. There were six sailors hitting him, Ed, and a couple others. Someone yelled the police were on their way, and the sailors left in a hurry. I understand Mountain told the cops a New Yorker was harassing one of his girls, and when he objected, the New Yorker and his Navy friends started to fight with him and his employees."

"They believed him?"

"There was no one to contradict his story. Ed, Pete, and some of the girls told the police that Mountain was telling the truth."

"Well, he got away with it, for now anyway."

"What do you mean 'for now, anyway'?"

Bobby looked at Jerry.

"Josephine, what I'm going to tell you can not be repeated. In fact, you'd better forget about our conversation, understand?"

"Yeah, okay. So what's going to happen?"

"I went to see my very special friend's buddies at the motel."

"I knew it! You have connections."

"Not me, it's my uncle's friends." Bobby winked at Jerry.

"So what did you tell them?"

"The truth. Mountain told them the same bullshit he told the police. I told them it was me dating Norma that got Mountain so pissed off that he hit me and the sailors came to my aid. They're going to investigate."

"Why, don't they believe you?"

"Josephine, Mountain works for them so they have to give him the benefit of the doubt. As for me, they have to believe that I wouldn't lie and embarrass my uncle, so they have to investigate."

"They can't possibly believe Mountain. Everyone knows he's a bully and a bastard."

"And, he likes to treat some of the girls like his personal property, right?"

"Yes, I told you that."

"Besides Norma, are there other girls that he bullied into staying even though they didn't want to?"

"Sure, Ellie and Jean are still here. Marilyn and Teressa finally left. I never heard from them again. Nobody ever questions Mountain. They're afraid of him."

"Josephine, this is important. When they come around to investigate, they will want to talk to you."

"Why me? They don't know me."

"They do now. I told them that you are a close friend of Norma's and how Mountain didn't like the idea of me seeing her. I also told them how she wanted to leave, but he doubled the amount of money she owed him."

"Can you believe he pulled that bullshit on her?"

"Yes I can, and they don't like that type of extortion being pulled on the girls. It's bad for morale. Besides the 'personal property' issue, the other main thing they're going to ask you about is the extra money Mountain wanted from Norma."

"I'll tell them, all right."

"And I didn't tell them you were lending her the money. I told them she had it saved."

"Okay. She really did have the money saved."

"And please don't worry. Mountain is more afraid of them than you are of Mountain, believe it or not. All they want is information."

"I'll tell them whatever they want to know."

"Honest?"

"Yes. I'm pissed about this whole dirty business that Mountain does."

"Great. Now, I need one more favor. Will you please call Norma and tell her that I'll be picking her up at six P.M., so we can spend our last night in New Orleans together in our private room?"

"Isn't she supposed to work to keep Mountain happy?"

Bobby couldn't wait to say this. "She doesn't work for Mountain anymore."

There was a long pause. "Did I understand what you just said to me?"

"That's right. She's free to go home."

"Oh my God, I can't believe it! How did you pull that one off?" she yelled.

"I told them how much she wanted to go back to her family and how hard Mountain was making it. So they let her go."

"I can't believe what you've done since you came here."

"I can't either. But I have my uncle to thank for it all. And remember, not one word about our conversation, my uncle, etc. etc. etc. If they find out, it will be bad for me, but sorry to say, much worse for you. Understand?"

"Of course. I've been around the block a few times. I know what's happening and what's not."

"Okay, now call Norma."

"One thing. What should she tell Mountain about not working tonight?"

"Tell her to call in sick. I'll tell her about her going home. Understand?"

"Yes, I'll call back after I talk to her. Oh yeah, what if she already went to work?"

"Never thought of that. You'll have to go and convince her to walk out with you. Let's worry about the details later. Let's just hope she's still home."

"She'll be so happy, especially after what happened to her last night."

"What happened to her last night, Josephine?"

Bobby could hear her sucking wind. "Mountain made her stay in his office for a few hours, according to one of the girls."

"To satisfy him?"

"I don't know. I didn't talk to her. But you can believe she didn't want to."

"That son of a bitch. I hope they nail his ass." Bobby realized what he had said. "But that's not my decision. Call me back, okay? Good-bye."

Bobby was upset. "That goddamn bastard Mountain."

"Are you going to tell Josephine about the 'servitude' issue?" Jerry asked.

"No. I believe John doesn't realize I picked up on it. I'm sure he would appreciate the less said about 'slave', the better. The main thing Josephine has to tell them is that Mountain treated some of his girls as his 'personal property,' like Norma. Right now, to John, it's the same thing."

"So there were other girls?"

"Yes, accordingly to Josephine, who should know. I'll just keep stressing this to her."

Five minutes later, Josephine called and told Bobby everything was in motion. Norma couldn't wait until six P.M. Bobby thanked her and finally got her phone number. He also gave her his home number.

"I'll be in touch with you before I leave."

"Promise?"

"Of course, one never lies to his good friends."

"Especially a very, very, special friend!" joked Josephine.

"And you are that. Talk to you soon. Bye."

Bobby took a painkiller and asked Jerry to wake him at four P.M. Except for a few hours nap, he was up for nearly thirty hours with no rest, just a lot of aggravation and some great news. He went to sleep immediately.

CHAPTER IX
THE END

The ringing telephone woke Bobby up. He looked at his wristwatch, and it was 3:30. Jerry wasn't around. Probably saying his good-byes to Sandy and M.J.

"Hello."

"Bobby, it's me, Josephine." She sounded a bit down and resigned.

"What's the matter?"

"Are you sitting down?"

"What happened?" Bobby was getting alarmed.

"Norma's in jail."

"*What?*" Bobby yelled.

"Norma and Mary Lou got arrested for shoplifting at Lords."

"Shoplifting what?"

"From the little news around here, it sounds like a dress."

"What the hell does she need another dress for? She looked great in that black one."

"Probably wanted something special for your last night together."

"Why didn't she pay for it?" Bobby asked.

"I don't know. Maybe she didn't have enough money. That's an expensive store."

"Is there a chance Mary Lou took the dress and Norma was just a bystander?"

"Norma could have been arrested as an accomplice. But why would Mary Lou need such a dress?" Josephine reasoned.

"Who knows?"

"We'll find out when Mountain and Norma get back to the bar."

"What's Mountain got to do with this?" Bobby growled.

"He went to bail her out."

"That's just great. Now he's a hero."

61

"She probably tried reaching me, but I was already on my way here."

Jerry walked in the room. "What's wrong? I heard you yell all the way down at the pool."

Bobby just shrugged and shook his head in disbelief.

"Josephine, please call me back when you have more information. Norma will probably come back with Mountain. Try to talk to her, okay?"

"All right. But don't worry too much. There's nothing we can do now."

"Yeah, bye."

Bobby looked at Jerry. "You're not going to believe this." He told him the news that Josephine just delivered.

"How can you figure this? She's free, but she's a jailbird?" Jerry wondered.

"Her stupid impulses," Bobby replied.

"You want something to eat?" Jerry said to change the subject.

"Yeah, a scotch and water. My stomach is in knots. I'll eat later."

Bobby started pacing the floor. "Mountain has his claws in her again, big time. Now it's bail money. He's going to look good protecting his girl by bailing her out."

"Bobby, you're confusing it. Yeah, he's helping her, but he's also in trouble because of the servitude issue. In fact, protecting her is part of the bondage." Jerry gave Bobby his drink.

"You're right. I just don't want him to get off the hook."

"No way. He's bad for business, and they know it, period."

"I sound like I'm getting paranoid. I'm also confused on why she took the dress."

"Did you tell her to mention to Norma that she was going to be free?"

"No. I told Josephine to tell her to call in sick and take the night off. I was planning on telling her when we were alone, tonight."

"Do you know if Josephine explained it that way, or did she, maybe, elaborate a little more?"

"I have to believe she did as she was told. Josephine knew I wanted to break the news personally."

"I'm just trying to find out if Norma got extra excited about this evening, as if she knew what you were going to tell her."

"Jerry, I'd like to believe that's what drove her to steal the dress, but I doubt it." Bobby started to get dressed. "Jerry, stay by the phone, please. I'm going to see if John is around. I've got to tell him what Norma pulled and how helpful Mountain was. Maybe he has some thoughts on what can be done to help get Norma out of this mess."

Bobby walked into the restaurant and went to the counter. The waitress smiled, "Hello, do you want to sit at the counter or at a table?"

"I'll take a table. Is John here?"

The waitress looked at Bobby. "Does he know you?"

"Yes. Please tell him Bobby's here."

"Well, he's not in yet, but he should be here any time now." She said as she looked at her watch.

"Okay. Please bring me a cup of coffee with cream." He went to the same table where he and John sat earlier this morning, around two A.M.

Bobby wondered what more information Josephine would have. There was still a chance he might see Norma tonight.

Bobby looked up just as John was walking in. The waitress waved John over, and she whispered in his ear while pointing in Bobby's direction. He looked over, nodded to her, said something, and walked over to Bobby. They shook hands.

"That's a nice looking bandage."

"Thank you for paying the doctor."

"What doctor?" John replied with a deadpan look.

Bobby just nodded his head, okay, and gave John a slight smile.

"What can I do for you?"

"I don't know how to tell you this, or try and explain it; it's so weird and so stupid." John just stared at Bobby. "Josephine called about an hour ago to tell me Norma got arrested for shoplifting a dress."

The waitress came over with the coffee. She served it and left.

John shook his head. "She really likes you."

Bobby was stunned at his mild reply.

John continued, "What store?"

"Lord's."

"That's an expensive shop. She probably picked out a dress that was too much for the money she had on her, so she gambled and lost. I'm sure she wanted that dress to impress you. After all, you're leaving tomorrow, right?"

"And, she got arrested."

"Because she loves you. You know, Bobby, you're an altar boy. An altar boy, not an angel. You see everything in black and white. An angel would be more forgiving. Norma's in the gray area, and you'll forgive her, to a point. But she's a thief, and that keeps you from seeing her white side. She did this for you, not for personal gain. Stupid? Yes, because she got caught. Otherwise, you'd have enjoyed the evening with her and her beautiful new dress. That's what she was looking forward to. That's what she gambled for. Don't beat her up for that. Don't walk in here and tell me you don't know how to explain it because it's so stupid, so weird. What you should have said was that she got arrested because she loves you. You don't deserve her."

Bobby just sat there, feeling like he was being scolded, which he was.

John was on a roll. "She would make a great wife. She would do anything you ask, do anything you want. And, she wouldn't ask you for special treatment. She loves you that much. The thing she dreads the most is to be an embarrassment to you."

"Well, I feel like an embarrassment to you. That's why I came in feeling that everything's screwed up. You helped get her to go home, and now she put herself in jail. And I understand what you're telling me. I'll try to convince her she's not an embarrassment to me."

"That's not going to happen."

"Why not?"

"She won't want to see you."

"Why?"

"You still don't get it. She's embarrassed, and that's the last thing she wants to face you with, an embarrassment."

"I'm willing to forgive and forget."

"I'm sure she figures that also, and that's what makes it so much harder for her to face you."

Bobby was shaking his head in disbelief.

"Bobby, listen, I could be wrong. Keep the evening open. Maybe you'll get together. But remember, after tonight, forget it all."

Bobby nodded his head in agreement, not wanting to really believe it. "Mountain posted bail for her."

"That's standard procedure. He has to show loyalty to the girls."

"I thought he just wanted to get his clutches into her some more."

John gave Bobby a smirk and shook his head, no.

"Is everything still on for her release from Mountain's grasp?"

"That hasn't changed."

"What about the extra money owed?"

"Let me worry about that."

"Thanks again, John. I'm sorry to have brought you such grief."

"In a way, it was a trade-off, and it wasn't all grief. A revelation for the most part."

Bobby knew what he meant. Mountain's servitude system was revealed to him before it could be exposed to all.

"What can be done about her shoplifting charge?"

"Well, it all depends if the store even presses charges. If they do, she'll need a lawyer, a good lawyer. Going to trial will be risky because Garrison is getting tough on crime, for even simple shoplifting cases, so they'll go for the throat. They want convictions."

"What are the options? Plead guilty now and hope to get probation?"

"No, the best thing would be for Lord's not to press charges, and the case is then dropped."

"How can that come about?"

"She must meet with them. It's important that this is her first offense. If not, then they'll consider her as habitual, and there's little chance that they'll listen to her story. Even worst, if she's a convicted shoplifter, then they will definitely want to press charges."

"I don't know for sure, but I can't believe she's done this before. What should she do, exactly?"

"Call and make an appointment with the store's manager. When they meet, it's up to her to convince him of her remorse, how she never did this before and that she'll never do it again. If given another chance, she'll walk the straight and narrow. In Norma's case, she wants to go back to her family and needs this break to help her get there. It's important that she be sincere and show it."

"She needs to practice what to say and how to say it," Bobby commented.

"She shouldn't go unless she has it all together. Josephine should help her because she knows her. She should also go with Norma to show the store manager that there's a witness to her statements, that there is someone who believes in her." John looked at Bobby and nodded. "That's it."

"I'll mention this to Josephine. And I don't want to beat a dead horse, but according to Josephine, after the beating incident, Mountain kept Norma locked in his office for hours. I'm sure they weren't playing cards." After saying that, Bobby realized his poor choice of words: "beat a dead horse."

John appeared to have noticed because he chuckled a little. "He was just collecting some of his interest, that's his way of thinking. Well, I've got to go."

They stood up and shook hands. "Take care of yourself, sonny."

"I'll try, and thank you, again."

Bobby didn't even check with the waitress about the bill, he just handed her $2 and thanked her. He went to a phone and called Jerry.

"Any calls?"

"Nothing."

"Want some dinner? I'll bring it back with me."

It was 5:30 when they finished their meal. Bobby changed his bandage and Jerry inspected the stitch job.

"Looks very good. He's a pro." Jerry gave his approval.

Finally, at six P.M. Josephine called.

"Bobby, she's okay."

"Not too shook up?"

"Of course she is. She said they treated her okay at the store, but the police rattled her. Believe it or not, she was happy to see Mountain."

"What about Mary Lou?"

"They let her go. Norma had the dress. Mary Lou played dumb. Smart girl."

"I'm sure her personality helped."

"Norma did try and reach me, but I was on my way to the bar, like I said before."

"How about Mountain?"

"He's not walking around beating his chest like he normally would. He seems subdued, very quiet. It's strange."

Bobby knew why. Somebody called him and told him to behave. Wait until the meeting—*Shazaam!*

"Did she say why she lifted the dress?"

"She went to Lords with Mary Lou because they were having a sale on dresses and accessories, you know, shoes, purses, and the like. She saw this charcoal gray-black dress, tried it on, and it fit perfectly. Mary Lou said she looked great. You already saw her black one and she wanted to surprise you. Even on sale, the dress was expensive. They didn't have enough money between them, and she didn't think she had enough time to go back home, return, and still make your date. So, she decided to take it and make amends later. She's done business with the store before and believed she could work it out. Turns out, she was wrong for not first discussing the situation with them."

"Norma's 'steal now and pay later' plan." Bobby shook his head.

"It was a dumb judgment call. Very dumb. She's paying for it now."

"Can I talk to Norma?"

"Bobby, I don't know how to tell you this. She is very happy you are okay."

"But?"

There was silence.

"She doesn't want to see you. She cried when I told her you were looking forward to meeting her tonight, but she doesn't want to see you."

"Is she blaming me because she took the dress for me?"

"Of course not. How could you think like that? She did what she did because she wanted to surprise you."

"Does she appear embarrassed?"

"That's a good explanation. It's like not wanting to face your father when you're get home from school because the school called to report a discipline problem."

God, John hit it on all cylinders.

"Will you please let her know I want to talk to her just this one time before I leave?"

"When are you leaving?"

"Since I won't be seeing her tonight, we'll be leaving tomorrow, Tuesday. Please bring her to the phone."

"I'll try."

Bobby waited a minute, but it seemed like an hour.

"Bobby, she doesn't want to talk to you. She's very upset. Maybe this weekend, after a few days have passed, she'll feel better."

"I hope so, Josephine. I'll call you noontime, Saturday, at your place. If she can't be there, get a number where I can call her. You have my home number. If anything important comes up, please call me."

"I will. I'm sorry the evening didn't go as planned. I'm also very sorry it all ended this way."

"The important thing is that she'll be free from Mountain."

"So, she is still scheduled to leave, thanks to your friends?"

"That's what I've been told; there's no change. But there is the problem of her arrest and possible conviction. That will really screw up her going home."

"What can be done to avoid that?"

"The best way out is for her to meet with the store manager and plead her case and her bad judgment call. I'm assuming this is her first offense, is that right?"

"I'm sure of that."

"Well, check it out with her. If she's been trouble-free, then she has a good chance to convince them this is a one-time thing. It's important that you practice with her, to get her to show remorse and a never-do-it-again attitude. She needs to stress wanting to go home to be with her children and mother. It's also important for you to go with her to show that she has someone who believes in her and can be a witness for her. If they don't press charges, the case will be dropped."

"I got it. I know what must be done. I'm going to miss you, Bobby."

"Same here. Thanks for being such a good friend to Norma, and to me, for the short time we knew each other."

"Too bad it was a short time—and, also, not a different time."

Bobby knew what she meant, and he agreed with her. She was a classy lady. "I understand."

"One last thing, do you know if they still want to talk to me?"

"Absolutely. That hasn't changed. Just answer their questions, and don't be nervous. They know you're a good friend to Norma. You know what to tell them, just the truth. We're depending on you."

"I'm not worried. We're trying to get Norma home. Thank you, and I know Norma thanks you, too."

"Okay. Take care, sweetheart. I'll be calling you Saturday. Good luck."

Bobby hung up. He couldn't continue the long good-bye. He started to cry.

The rest of the evening was spent packing and calling home. They had something to eat at eight. Bobby remembered he forgot to tell the manager he didn't need the extra room. Too late now. Bobby and Jerry hardly spoke. Jerry knew Bobby was hurting and not because of the cut over his eye. When they got back to the room, the phone was ringing. It was Josephine.

"Hello. I've been trying to get you since I got home. I didn't want to leave a message."

"What's happening?"

"Mountain called me into his office just before I was ready to leave. He asked me to take Norma home. Then he told me to show up for an eleven A.M. meeting in his office tomorrow."

"Did he say why?"

"No, just a meeting. He didn't say who would be there. He gave me ten dollars for the cab ride. That's a first. On the way, Norma was wondering about my meeting. I told her it was because I challenged a bar bill and it did not involve her."

"Good girl. Did Mountain tell her to show up tomorrow, too?"

"Yes, he did. He told her to be at work at noon. He did not mention a meeting with her."

"I'm sure there will be one. Your meeting should be over by noontime. Well, the wheels are in motion. It's up to you; don't screw it up."

"I won't. Believe me, I'm looking forward to it."

"Please Josephine, don't get cocky. This is serious business. Don't give any indication you know anything about the meeting. Do you understand?"

"I understand. I'll be serious and sincere and tell them whatever they want to know. Don't worry, Bobby."

"Did Norma ask about me?"

"Of course. I told her you were going to call me on Saturday afternoon to find out where she could be reached, to talk to her. She started crying again."

"All right, enough. After tomorrow, if all goes well, Norma should be unemployed. No more Club Paree and Mountain."

"I hope so. God, I hope so."

"Listen, I'll call you tomorrow night from wherever we land, figure about nine P.M. Is that okay?"

"Sure, I'll have a full report."

"Get a good night's sleep, and good luck tomorrow."

"Yes. Good night Bobby."

Bobby discussed the conversation with Jerry. They fell asleep around eleven.

They got up at six A.M., finished packing, had breakfast, said good-bye to Helen, told her to give John their regards, paid the hotel bill, and headed for home.

They decided not to go back through Memphis. Part was to see something different. The other reason was that Bobby didn't want to see the gang. Too much to discuss about the bandage and what caused the damage.

Two items struck them on their trip. One was the cardboard shacks they saw on some of the farms in the deep South. The other was the "dry" and "wet" counties they drove through. Signs on the border side of "wet" counties would warn: 50 MILES OF "DRY" UNTIL YOU GET TO THE NEXT "WET" COUNTY. GET YOUR BEER HERE."

Bobby called Josephine as planned on Tuesday night from his motel room just outside Atlanta.

"Bobby, it went as discussed. It was like a dream come true. Everything fell right into place." Josephine was ecstatic.

A man named Nick asked her questions. They were alone. She answered him as simply as possible and only got excited, and emotional, when they talked about Norma's money issue and her concern for Norma's future. She told Nick about Mountain wanting to "collect dolls," as Nick described Mountain's hobby. It was a colorful term for servitude. She mentioned Marilyn and Teressa as old "dolls" and Ellie and Jean as current ones, like Norma. Nick was very polite. He never pushed her or questioned the sincerity of her answers, and he thanked her when they finished.

"I felt great when I left the office. But it got even better. Norma was called into Mountain's office to meet with Nick. It was about one P.M. I was sitting at the bar talking to Norma when she got the call. When she got out of the meeting, she was so excited, I didn't know what to think. Then she told me what happened. Nick told her he was informed that she wanted to go back home to her family. He never mentioned the four hundred dollars owed. He wished her luck and gave her a bonus because she was such a loyal employee. Bobby, he gave her eight hundred dollars. Norma said she nearly fainted. She said her good-byes to everyone, cleaned out her locker, and I took her home in a cab. She was still shaking, not fully believing she was free from Mountain. She gave me back four hundred dollars and wanted to give me one hundred dollars extra, but I refused." Josephine paused to light a cigarette. "It was then that I told her we had to plead her case to the Lord's store manager so that she wouldn't go to jail. I'm meeting her tomorrow to go over everything. I'll call the manager and arrange a meeting on Thursday."

"That's great. They lived up to their pledge to let Norma go, but the eight hundred dollars was unexpected. John said they would take care of the money owed, but not this. I'm happy for her. This will give her something more to live on until she finds the right job."

"Bobby, she's in utter disbelief. We knew what was possibly going to happen, but this bonus money came out of nowhere."

"Josephine, she must never know the details. All she must know is that Mountain's boss felt sorry for her predicament. That's it. Nothing more. Got it?"

"Yes, I understand."

"So, practice well and everything will go well. You did a great job today, Josephine. It had to feel good."

"Like I said, it was like a fantasy come true. Everything fell into place."

"I expect good news when I call you on Saturday. Thank you, Josephine, and get a good night's rest."

"Don't worry, Bobby, I will. Good night."

They got home Friday, late afternoon. They had a minor car problem in Maryland. The car needed a new distributor cap. It cost them nearly a day. Bobby stopped in to visit Jerry's parents and to have Doc check the wound. When he finally got home, Bobby called his mother in Pennsylvania and Lila around the corner. He later went over to see her. He told her about slipping at the pool, hitting his head, and needing stitches. That was the same story he told everyone. Otherwise, the trip was not extraordinary, except for the food and music and seeing everyone in Memphis.

On Saturday, at one P.M., Bobby called Josephine.

"I hope you have nothing but good news to report."

"It's as good as it was on Tuesday."

"How's that?"

"Well, to begin with, Mountain is gone. Nick announced that he was the new club manager, and Mountain retired to his hometown of Baton Rouge. We didn't have the chance to give him a farewell party, damn it!"

"You love it, don't you? How about Ed and Charlie?"

"Charlie got promoted to Ed's nighttime shift, and Ed took over the day shift with less patrons and less money. Poor dear."

"How did that happen?"

"I mentioned it to Nick during our meeting. It was an answer to one of his questions about which one was the better bartender."

"And that's all it took to demote Ed?"

"I have the feeling they knew Ed was a complainer and too greedy. Charlie has the better personality and is a better bartender. All I did was confirm that."

"Good for Charlie. He deserves the promotion. Any other changes?"

"No. Jean and Ellie are still here. They decided to stay with the new management. I'm sure they also got a bonus. They deserve it."

"Why did Mountain select these girls?"

"They're all like Norma. Very pretty and sweet."

"Just the opposite of Mountain."

"Exactly."

"How is Norma?"

"I thought you'd never ask. Norma is back home."

"You're kidding!" Bobby yelled.

"Nope."

"So the meeting with the store manager was a success."

"Bobby, Norma was terrific. She poured her heart out. She showed him pictures of her boys and said all of the right, remorseful things. He said he understood, but he needed to contact his supervisors and discuss it with them. He said he would call us later that day. I gave him my number. We waited, and at three P.M. he told us they would not press charges against Norma, but she was never to visit the store again. They also wished her luck!"

Josephine paused to take a drag on her cigarette. Bobby wondered if John had assisted in the store's decision. He would never know.

"Norma cried. So did I. She called her mother and told her she was coming home by bus on Friday. She packed that night, only her clothes and personal items. She left her books, a lamp, and a television for me to bring up the next time I visit by car. She left Mary Lou with all the furniture and stuff. She showed me the picture of you two at Pete Fountain's. She was in love with it. I told her you wanted me to buy something special from you, but I never got it. She said the picture was special enough."

"Did she say when I could call her?"

Josephine was silent, only taking a drag on her cigarette.

"Bobby, it's over."

Bobby sighed. "I guessed it would be. I was hoping for a change of heart. I wanted to talk to her one last time, to wish her well."

"She knows that. Please don't think about it anymore. Just end it all, now."

"You're right. Thank you for being such a good friend. Tell Norma I wish her only the best and the same for you. Take care, Josephine."

"You too, Bobby." And they hung up.

EPILOGUE

On the way back, Bobby and Jerry naturally discussed the trip. The good and the bad. The music. The places. The people. The characters. The strange twists and all that excitement and intrigue in just a week. From Monday to Sunday. One beating to another.

Bobby thought of Norma's dynamite kisses. Little did they realize that their last kiss would be Norma's peck on Bobby's cheek, the last time they were together, the night after the picnic.

"Making love with Norma was special."

"That's what we expected from the girls in New Orleans." Jerry smiled.

"Funny," Bobby replied. "That's what she said at the picnic. She really did, Jerry."

"Where did you learn that expression?"

"At work. My boss, Ted, said that to me in reply to a casual comment I made, something like, 'Work stinks.'"

Bobby realized that if he ever wrote a book on the trip that would have to be the title. It was apropos.

Bobby knew there was one person who made the whole trip worthwhile. The one person who was the difference between Norma going home to Natchez and Norma languishing in the Club Paree. That person was the cabdriver. He had told Bobby about the management at the Town and Country. How this information was acted on was secondary. Without this knowledge, nothing noteworthy would have been accomplished. An honorary mention had to be District Attorney Garrison. His "get-tough-on-crime" stance made John release Norma.

Bobby remembered another time when a cabdriver's observation was right on target, a few years earlier. In the summer of 1959, Bobby was best man at his friend Frank's wedding to Martha in Havana, Cuba. Castro had just come into power and was on good terms with the United

States. Bobby took pictures with the armed guerilla's who roamed the streets in their camouflage uniforms. They were very friendly. A few pictures were taken with them in a big plaza in front of the enormous statue of the revolutionary hero, Jose Marti. During one cab ride, Bobby had a conversation with the driver, who was aware of what was happening around him, like the cabby in New Orleans. Bobby asked him about the changes since Castro had taken over. He replied that the main change was the people being much happier not living under the Baptista regime. The tourists still came for the weather, the relatively cheap vacation, and the beautiful hotels with their extravagant shows and gambling, if one was so inclined. He commented that the Superman show was still a big draw; the man with the twelve-inch-plus "ying-yang." The cabby also mentioned, in a casual way, that there were many more European men now visiting who spoke in an eastern European language, like Russian or Polish. They never spoke in Spanish or English. The only words the cabdriver understood were the general ones, "Castro," "America," and the like. Bobby didn't think much about the cabby's comments until Castro announced in 1960 that he was a Communist. Then, it all made sense.

There was another ominous aspect about their trip—not directly, but just the fact they were in New Orleans the year before JFK was assassinated. There were Louisiana connections: Lee Harvey Oswald, Jack Ruby, and many others. Bobby and Jerry wondered how many of them they passed on the streets or rubbed shoulders in the same bar or restaurant. Jim Garrison eventually wrote a book about an assassination/conspiracy theory involving the government and the CIA. The book was based on his attempt as district attorney, in the late 1960s, to prosecute one Clay Shaw as a conspirator with the government. Bobby looked at all the faces and places pictured in the newspapers, magazines, and on television. He never recognized any of them, thank God. That would have really given him the willies.

After that Saturday conversation, Bobby never spoke with Josephine again. He often thought of her and, of course, Norma, whom he would never forget. He assumed all went well in their lives, but would Josephine ever call him with bad news?

Later in the summer of 1962, August, the other Norma died.

Bobby married the girl from Brooklyn, Joan (Bubbles), and had a son and two daughters.

Jerry married a girl from Long Island, Stacia, and had a son.

They both lived to collect Social Security.